"Some horror walks you down a dark corridor, where there's whispers and laughter, sobs and screams. Other horror starts down at the end of that corridor, where there's a door that opens on to you don't know what. Read this, and then decide where Eric LaRocca has left you. Not that it matters. There's no way out."
Stephen Graham Jones, author of *The Only Good Indians* and *My Heart is a Chainsaw*

"Eric LaRocca's unflinching *Things Have Gotten Worse Since We Last Spoke* will crawl inside you, move stuff around, and make you see the world differently, like all great stories do."
Paul Tremblay, author of *A Head Full of Ghosts* and *The Pallbearers Club*

"A startling affair... I'll be cleaning up particles of darkness in my office for weeks."
Josh Malerman, author of *Bird Box* and *Malorie*

"Bleak, clever, edgy, and vicious. Eric LaRocca draws his readers in for something they will never expect and never forget."
Sadie Hartmann, 'Mother Horror'

"LaRocca's combination of structure, adept pacing and masterful language is more complex than meets the eye... A must-read for fans of body horror, epistolary novels, and depravity."
Library Journal

THINGS
HAVE
GOTTEN
WORSE
SINCE
WE LAST
SPOKE

AND OTHER
MISFORTUNES

ERIC LaROCCA

THINGS HAVE GOTTEN WORSE SINCE WE LAST SPOKE

AND OTHER MISFORTUNES

TITAN BOOKS

Things Have Gotten Worse Since We Last Spoke
and Other Misfortunes
Hardback edition ISBN: 9781803361499
Signed edition ISBN: 9781803363141
Paperback edition ISBN: 9781803363769
E-book edition ISBN: 9781803361505

Published by Titan Books
A division of Titan Publishing Group Ltd
144 Southwark Street, London SE1 0UP

First edition: September 2022
3 4 5 6 7 8 9 10

A CIP catalogue record for this title is available
from the British Library.

Printed and bound by CPI Group (UK) Ltd,
Croydon, CR0 4YY.

For Ali, my love.
Things have gotten better since we first met.
You make me feel like less of a monster.

CONTENTS

THINGS
HAVE
GOTTEN
WORSE
SINCE
WE LAST
SPOKE

AUTHOR'S NOTE

As there has already been an overwhelming amount of conjecture and vitriol—especially in the dominion of online discussion—regarding the untimely demise of Agnes Petrella at the age of twenty-four, the author of this text has tenderly and judiciously compiled the following content with the hope of enlightening the public by publishing the contents of her correspondence with Zoe Cross in the several months prior to her death.

Because the litigation surrounding Zoe Cross's case remains open at the time of this publication, certain elements of their communication have been redacted or censored at the behest of the Henley's Edge Police Department. The author has noticeably marked these redacted elements with [omitted]. The absent contents remain in the archives of the Henley's Edge Police Department and are strictly forbidden from being removed from their records.

The author wishes to extend their heartfelt gratitude to the Henley's Edge Police Department, specifically Captain Gregory Deacon and Judge Louis Urchek for their amenableness and unwavering support throughout the course of composing this publication.

Also, the author of this publication requests that the reader be cognizant of the fact that the author is in no way affiliated with either Zoe Cross's legal counsel or Agnes Petrella's surviving family. The author remains a nonpartisan entity and instead patiently waits for the balances of justice to tip in favor of the truth.

PART ONE

A SLICED APPLE

POST WRITTEN BY AGNES PETRELLA ON ONLINE QUEER COMMUNITY BOARD

[The following post was recovered from QueerList.org—a website where members, usually openly identifying members of the LGBTQ+ community, can converse and solicit. The author wishes to express their heartfelt gratitude to the website's chief administrator, Sig Thornton, for recovering the post from his well-organized archives and for being so remarkably generous throughout the research process.]

Antique Apple Peeler with Vibrant History for Sale
Date: Friday, May 26, 2000 at 3:47 p.m. EST
User: agnes_in_wonderland_76
Asking Price: $250 (will settle for $220)

I was going to begin this with some absurd comment about the irony of posting about an apple peeler in a queer discussion forum when most of us are probably upset by the mere mention of the word "fruit."

I decided to begin with a story instead.

Every family has a myth for the young to inherit—an undocumented fable passed between mouths, a grave illness to be contracted—as if the very words were a blight to infect the youth with and let them know they're now welcome to the fold.

After all, what exactly is a family, if not a brotherhood and sisterhood afflicted with the same terminal disease?

When I was very young, my grandmother told me a story about how her mother—an immigrant from Naples—had desperately longed for a proper apple peeler in order to make a traditional apple pie.

The man she had married, though generous enough to gift her five children to carry in her belly over the course of six years, was resolute in his decision—he would not give her the money for the apple peeler no matter how much she begged.

So, my great-grandmother devised a plan to make her husband understand just how urgently she needed a peeler. Not only would her plan showcase her need, but it would stress a measure of safety as well.

The following day, my great-grandmother packed her husband's lunch pail and kissed him "goodbye" as he set off for work. She waited, spent the morning tailoring a suit for one of her neighbors. Finally, the news she had been waiting for arrived. One of the Carpino boys that lived next door showed up on her doorstep and explained how her husband had been taken to the local doctor.

"What for?" she had asked, her hands hiding the smile beginning to thaw across her face.

"Something he ate," the Carpino boy told her. "He bit into an apple with a sewing needle stuck inside."

A week later and my great-grandmother was at the local department store picking out an apple peeler, chaperoned by her dear husband with his jaw bandaged shut.

As you can already tell by the pictures attached to this thread [images omitted], this antique apple peeler has endured for over a century and provided sustenance for four generations of family members.

I've gone through various documents my grandmother had left me and consequently discovered a letter my great-grandmother had sent to her sister (who was living in Turin, Italy at the time) and she details going to the department store with her husband to pick out an apple peeler. The letter is dated August 5th, 1897. So, that means, in no uncertain terms, the apple peeler was manufactured in 1897. Possibly even earlier—1896. I can happily scan a copy of the letter and include it with the item for the sake of verifying the appliance's authenticity. I'm also more than happy to send along a copy of the letter for a historian to verify prior to purchase.

You might be interested to know not only was the apple peeler's purchase of the sordid variety, but the appliance furnished the hands of one of the state of Connecticut's beloved composers—Charles Ives. My grandmother, frequently guilty of repeating the same story at a family gathering on separate occasions, would often regale those who were patient enough to listen more than once with the story of how the apple peeler was once used by Charles Ives, a family friend, at a picnic in 1948—the very year after he had won the Pulitzer Prize.

Unfortunately, there's no way to authenticate this claim that the apple peeler was once used by Mr. Ives. On two separate occasions, I have scoured my parents' basement in search of photographs documenting the picnic and found no evidence of Mr. Ives at a family picnic in the late 1940s.

In an effort to be as transparent with you as possible, my grandmother was prone to manufacturing stories that she imagined might titillate her guests. She once told a family friend that Marcello Mastroianni (you might remember him from *La Dolce Vita*) was a distant family relation on her mother's side. Her stories became more fanciful and varied in her old age; however, she clung to the story of Charles Ives until the night the hospice nurses arrived.

Make of that what you will.

If you're in the market for a conversation starter, then look no further. I can't tell you the amount of times house guests have marveled at this particular antique appliance pinned to my kitchen wall. On more than three separate occasions I've had offers from guests to purchase the peeler; however, at the time, I couldn't bear to part with it.

If you're a serious collector with a fervent taste for traditional Americana—no pun intended—then this is the appliance for you. Be mindful that this appliance is still in proper working order. Though, a skilled owner will be aware not to overuse the tool as it requires the tenderness only a true collector possesses. It's my sincere hope that this apple peeler will go to a considerate and thoughtful owner, eager to add a touch of history to their beautiful home, or perhaps to add another excellent addition to their growing collection.

Feel free to email me: agnes_in_wonderland_76@[omitted]. com with any further questions. I'm delighted to help in any way I can. Please do not contact me with unsolicited services or offers.

Please be advised, once purchased I will not accept returns or issue refunds.

EMAIL FROM ZOE CROSS

[The following pages contain the first correspondence between Zoe Cross and Agnes Petrella. As mentioned in the Author's Note, certain sections of the email correspondence have been truncated or omitted entirely as Ms. Cross's case is still pending an investigation.]

Date: 05/28/2000
Time: 12:09 p.m.
From: Zoe Cross <crushedmarigolds@[omitted].com>
To: Agnes Petrella <agnes_in_wonderland_76@[omitted].com>
Subject: Re: Antique Apple Peeler with Vibrant History for Sale

Dear Agnes,

While I don't claim to possess the refinement of a serious antique collector, I'm filled with the same urgency of your great-grandmother to acquire something very near and dear to my heart. My grandfather is turning ninety-two during the month of July. He's especially fond of the work of composer Charles Ives and, quite frankly, I had to do a double take when I first read your original post because it seemed too serendipitous—too good to be true.

Although it's unfortunate you can't prove the appliance was once in the possession of Mr. Ives at a family picnic, I think my grandfather would be tickled to know of the story and would appreciate the appliance with or without the proper proof.

My grandfather, a World War Two veteran, doesn't talk much about his involvement with the war; however, he has mentioned time and time again how the lieutenants in the garrisons would often play Ives on the radio. In fact, one of my earliest memories of my grandfather—other than his distinct smell of lavender—involves me sitting on his lap on the front porch of his house in Revere, MA, as a Charles Ives record played.

I understand in your original post you had stressed the importance of the appliance going to the home of a serious collector. Unfortunately, I cannot pretend to claim my grandfather is a dedicated collector. In fact, with his health failing, it's more than likely that the appliance will be in his possession for a few years—maybe even months if his current doctor's prognosis proves to be true—before it's inherited by one of the younger members of our family. Possibly myself.

That's not to say that my grandfather does not covet his belongings with the tenderness and care of an antiquarian specialist. My grandfather recently purchased a Harpers Ferry Model 1855 musket at a public auction in Danvers, MA. He's since cared for the rifle as if it were his only child. I visit him occasionally on the weekends when I can comfortably make the trek from Cambridge to Springfield and typically find him hunched over his prized possession, hands furiously polishing the barrel with a cloth.

If you were to sell the antique apple peeler to me—and I wholeheartedly understand if you carry some reservations given the questionable longevity of my grandfather's health—I can assure you the appliance will be well looked after. If not by my grandfather, then by me personally. As I have explained, I don't pretend to be an antique specialist; however, I can assure you I make good word of my promises. Of course, you're more than likely hesitant to accept such a statement from a perfect stranger on the internet. Regardless, the apple peeler will be finding a good home.

If you haven't tossed my email in the trash by now, perhaps we could discuss the matter of the price. According to your post, you're seeking $250, but will settle for $220. I think that's more than agreeable given the rich history surrounding the appliance. After all, it's still in working order!

Would you be receptive to offering express shipping at no additional cost if I offered to pay the desired $250? It would certainly help my pocketbook.

Of course, I completely understand if that's not possible. We can negotiate later.

Regardless, please let me know if you are open to the idea of selling the apple peeler to me. I would be more than delighted to take it off your hands and offer it the best home I can afford.

I look forward to hearing from you.

Best regards,
Zoe

EMAIL FROM AGNES PETRELLA

Date: 05/29/2000

Time: 10:43 a.m.

From: Agnes Petrella <agnes_in_wonderland_76@[omitted].com>

To: Zoe Cross <crushedmarigolds@[omitted].com>

Subject: Re: Antique Apple Peeler with Vibrant History for Sale

Dear Zoe,

Thank you so much for reaching out and for writing such a thoughtful email. Most of the responses I've been receiving on the post have unfortunately been solicitations for activities I can't even imagine having the determination to write down, let alone engage in. Your email was a much welcome respite from a seemingly never-ending onslaught of rudeness.

So, thank you for that.

Based on the thoughtfulness of your email and the dedication you put into crafting your inquiry, I am most certainly open to the idea of selling you the apple peeler. Although my original post may have stressed the importance of the new owner possessing a certain skillset in order to appropriately take care of the appliance, much of that was said in order to suitably vet the contacts who might attempt to query me.

As you can probably tell from my original post, this apple peeler means a great deal to me. It's been in my family for many generations and was passed down to me by my mother. If possible, I would like for it to become a treasured item belonging to another family—a precious relic to become a birthright for a new generation. I don't anticipate having children of my own, so I would hope that the apple peeler might go to a home burgeoning with little ones. Of course, I understand this may not be possible. Despite my wishes, I think your grandfather would take excellent care of the apple peeler.

If you'd like, I would be happy to include a small note in the parcel detailing my grandmother's account of Charles Ives at the family picnic. I only wish I could prove the report. But, as you said, your grandfather will appreciate the appliance with or without the proof.

To answer your question regarding express shipping at no additional cost, I would be more than happy to offer to send the parcel at an expedited rate at no additional cost if you purchase the item at the requested $250. I think that would be more than agreeable. Plus, I hardly expected I would find somebody as caring and as devoted to their family as you.

It's my pleasure to sell the apple peeler to you, especially knowing how fond your grandfather is of Charles Ives. Isn't that perfect?

I must admit, I'm slightly hesitant to sell the appliance in general considering how precious it has been to me over the years. It's really the only thing my mother has ever given me. Not to mention, it's something my grandmother touted as a magical instrument when I was little. I used to foolishly think it could grant wishes.

I guess we all have things from our childhood we eventually must let go of.

Please send me your mailing address after you've sent the payment and we'll go from there.

Again, thank you so much for your thoughtfulness. It means so much to me.

Best regards,
Agnes

EMAIL FROM ZOE CROSS

Date: 05/29/2000

Time: 3:13 p.m.

From: Zoe Cross <crushedmarigolds@[omitted].com>

To: Agnes Petrella <agnes_in_wonderland_76@[omitted].com>

Subject: Re: Antique Apple Peeler with Vibrant History for Sale

Dear Agnes,

I am overjoyed to know you're willing to sell me the apple peeler, especially with the requested expedited shipping at no additional cost. I was hesitant—perhaps nervous as well—to send you my initial email as I worried I wouldn't be an adequate candidate for your item, but I'm so delighted to hear you're receptive to my offer.

I plan to send the money to your bank tomorrow afternoon when the funds appear in my account after I make the necessary transfer.

I hope you'll excuse my momentary forwardness with you, but I'm curious to know why you're selling the apple peeler in the first place if it holds such profound emotional value to you. I have to admit—I'm hesitant to make the purchase of the item if you're on the fence about selling.

I would hate to think I'm robbing you of some dearly cherished, irreplaceable artifact.

Best,
Zoe

EMAIL FROM AGNES PETRELLA

Date: 05/30/2000

Time: 8:32 a.m.

From: Agnes Petrella <agnes_in_wonderland_76@[omitted].com>

To: Zoe Cross <crushedmarigolds@[omitted].com>

Subject: Re: Antique Apple Peeler with Vibrant History for Sale

Zoe,

I sincerely appreciate your thoughtfulness during this difficult time. I don't consider your email to be too forward at all, considering how vulnerable I made myself during my original online post. I wholeheartedly understand your concern to purchase now, especially after I've expressed how precious the appliance was—and still is—to me and my family.

The truth is this apple peeler is one of the few things I have left of my grandmother. She passed away when I was a teenager and had always joked that this apple peeler was to serve as my dowry. When I moved out on my own—into my first apartment—it was one of the few things my mother could afford to give me as a housewarming present. Something I had treasured for so many years—a reminder of the generous and beautiful spirit my grandmother once was.

That night, my mother and I peeled apples to make a pie. We ate cookies with vanilla frosting until two in the morning.

The fact is that was the last night my mother and I laughed together. Or even hugged, for that matter.

You see, when I left home for the first time, I made a promise to myself that I would live as authentically as I possibly could. No matter the consequences.

So, I did.

I picked up the phone and I called my mom and I said, "Mom, there's something I need to tell you and Dad."

She exhaled; the dim rumbling of her breath clogging in the pit of her throat sounded like a thunderstorm breaking apart as it passed through a stretch of mountains.

I waited until I could hear my father milling about in the background, close enough to hear what I had to say.

Finally, I said it: "Mom, Dad. I'm gay."

There was a long, painful pause, and I recall I could feel my heartbeat hammering in the space between my ears—the blood rushing to my face and pooling there.

Finally, my mother spoke. "My child isn't gay."

And she hung up.

That was the very last thing she said to me. I haven't talked to her in two years.

The apple peeler was one of the last things she gave me before we stopped talking—something I thought I would keep as a memory of my family until I had a family of my own one day. But that doesn't seem that likely anymore.

You had asked me why exactly I was selling the apple peeler if it held such a profound sentimental value. The truth is, I would keep it if I could. I don't want to bore you with the details or throw myself a little pity party, but I've been struggling to make my rent payment for the last several months because of a pay cut I had to take at my job. The extra $250 would really help me out this coming month and keep me afloat so I can bide my time before I can figure out what I'm going to do next.

I had never planned to reveal exactly why I was planning to sell the apple peeler to whoever I arranged to purchase the item. But you seem so genuine and so thoughtful. I know you won't judge me or think ill of me for discarding such a precious remnant of my family's history.

I assure you I would never accept your money if I knew in my heart I could not bear to part with it. More importantly, I promise not to pester you after the purchase and make certain the apple peeler is being well cared for. Once we make the transaction, that's it. I trust that the apple peeler will be going to a good home with you and your grandfather. I have no reservations to sell. If it seems like I am somewhat hesitant, it's merely because it feels like I'm holding a funeral for my former self—the person I was before I lived with integrity and honesty. It's the funeral for a person I wouldn't want you to know.

After all, I much prefer who I am now.

Well, sometimes I do.

Although I must confess—I sometimes wonder how I'll properly peel apples without it. I suppose the Greek philosopher, Epicurus, was right—"A free life cannot acquire many possessions, because this is not easy to do without servility to mobs or monarchs."

Best,
Agnes

EMAIL FROM ZOE CROSS

Date: 05/31/2000
Time: 9:24 a.m.
From: Zoe Cross <crushedmarigolds@[omitted].com>
To: Agnes Petrella <agnes_in_wonderland_76@[omitted].com>
Subject: Re: Antique Apple Peeler with Vibrant History for Sale

Agnes,

Once again, I hope you'll excuse my forwardness when I ask for your bank account routing information so that I can wire your monthly rent payment to you. I know we don't even really know one another, but I recognize when I've been blessed with certain things others have not.

I would be remiss if I did not take this opportunity to help you in the way that you so clearly need. I'm lucky enough to never have to worry about rent payment or whether or not I'll survive another bill cycle, and I would be honored to help you do the same.

I know you'll probably be hesitant—you'll probably insist that you don't need the assistance. I would ask you to reconsider your stubbornness and accept help when it's offered so freely and so selflessly.

I would also like to take this opportunity to give you my Instant Messenger contact information in case you ever need to talk. You can find me at <crushedmarigolds>. I'm usually online later at night as I typically work during the day.

Please never hesitate to reach out or ask for help if you need it. As I said before, I know we're complete strangers to one another, but I truly believe I'm within my right to help another human being when I can see clearly that they're struggling.

Talk soon,
Zoe

EMAIL FROM AGNES PETRELLA

Date: 05/31/2000
Time: 11:12 a.m.
From: Agnes Petrella <agnes_in_wonderland_76@[omitted].com>
To: Zoe Cross <crushedmarigolds@[omitted].com>
Subject: Re: Antique Apple Peeler with Vibrant History for Sale

Zoe,

I'm so shocked by your generosity. I really don't quite know what to say. I've, of course, heard of things like this happening to people. But never in my wildest dreams did I ever think it would happen to me.

Normally I would pretend to resist slightly or make up some nonsensical excuse as to why I couldn't possibly accept your offer.

I'm afraid I'm at such a loss for words I can barely think of anything to say other than "yes."

I'm a bit hesitant to give out my private information over email, but I know full well you won't be able to rob me. There's hardly anything left in my account. I spent all I had left yesterday on groceries for the rest of the week.

I didn't know how I was going to pay the month of June's

rent, to be frank. It was the first time in my life I had thought of doing horrible things to actually get a paycheck.

My bank routing information is as follows:

[omitted]

Once again, I don't quite know what to say.

I've been called many things over the years, but "speechless" has seldom been one of them. I don't quite know what I could ever do to repay you for your kindness, but I'll think of something. Maybe we'll be able to meet up one day so I can properly thank you in person.

Again, thank you for your kindness. It means so much to me.

Your friend,
Agnes

EMAIL FROM AGNES PETRELLA

Date: 06/01/2000
Time: 10:46 a.m.
From: Agnes Petrella <agnes_in_wonderland_76@[omitted].com>
To: Zoe Cross <crushedmarigolds@[omitted].com>
Subject: THANK YOU!

THANK YOU FROM THE BOTTOM OF MY HEART!

I just called my bank and they notified me that the total sum of one thousand dollars had been wired to my account last night by a Ms. Zoe Cross.

I don't quite know what to say.

I never thought anything like this would ever happen in my life.

I owe you so much. I can't believe this is real.

Thank you. A million times.

Your friend,
Agnes xoxo

EMAIL FROM AGNES PETRELLA

Date: 06/01/2000
Time: 11:07 a.m.
From: Agnes Petrella <agnes_in_wonderland_76@[omitted].com>
To: Zoe Cross <crushedmarigolds@[omitted].com>
Subject: Re: THANK YOU!

OK. I've calmed down since I sent my last email. Hopefully this one will be more coherent.

I really do owe you so much for your kindness, your generosity, etc.

I truly never thought something like this would ever happen to me. I don't have to go to bed tonight dreading tomorrow—waking up in a cold sweat and wondering if my check will bounce.

You really have changed my life.

I don't know what I could possibly ever do to repay you, but just know that you have changed the life of someone who was seriously contemplating ending it all if things kept going the way they were going.

It's not as if I had a plan or anything. I didn't go out and buy a rope or rat poison to stir in my morning coffee. But I was sincerely considering doing something to change my life in an irreversible way. You plucked me right from the edge before I was about to jump. I hope you know that.

I really can't thank you enough for what you've given me. You've changed my life, guardian angel.

Your friend,
Agnes xoxo

EMAIL FROM ZOE CROSS

Date: 06/01/2000
Time: 2:39 p.m.
From: Zoe Cross <crushedmarigolds@[omitted].com>
To: Agnes Petrella <agnes_in_wonderland_76@[omitted].com>
Subject: Re: THANK YOU!

Agnes,

Of course. It was my sincere pleasure.

I would be more than happy to lend a helping hand anytime you find yourself in a bind. This is not merely a one-time offer.

When you're gay, you have the privilege of choosing your family.

I learned quickly that blood is not always thicker than water. Sometimes the people that care for us the most are the people we least expect.

I, like you, have a responsibility to my fellow queer brothers and sisters to aid them with my blessings.

If you'd like to talk, I'll be on Instant Messenger tonight. We can talk more there.

Your friend,
Zoe

INSTANT MESSAGING CONVERSATION BETWEEN AGNES AND ZOE

[The following text is a transcript of a conversation between Agnes Petrella and Zoe Cross over Instant Messenger. Certain sections of the text have been censored or redacted at the request of the Henley's Edge Police Department. These censored areas have been marked with [omitted].]

06/01/2000

[<crushedmarigolds> has entered the chat]
[<agnes_in_wonderland_76> has entered the chat]

10:09:04 <crushedmarigolds> Hey

10:09:13 <agnes_in_wonderland_76> Hey

10:09:19 <agnes_in_wonderland_76> I came earlier, but you weren't on yet

10:09:29 <crushedmarigolds> Yeah, sorry. I was out for a bit. Couldn't get to the computer. Here now

10:09:40 <agnes_in_wonderland_76> I'm glad

10:10:01 <crushedmarigolds> Did you send the rent check to your landlord?

10:10:13 <agnes_in_wonderland_76> Took it to the post office this afternoon

10:10:23 <crushedmarigolds> Good. I'm glad

10:10:34 <agnes_in_wonderland_76> I really can't thank you enough

10:10:45 <crushedmarigolds> You think he'll be surprised?

10:10:57 <agnes_in_wonderland_76> I'm sure he was busy writing my eviction notice

10:11:22 <crushedmarigolds> You must be delighted to prove him wrong

10:11:48 <agnes_in_wonderland_76> I can't stop smiling. One of the women I worked with said she had never seen me happier

10:11:56 <crushedmarigolds> I'm glad you're so happy

10:12:09 <agnes_in_wonderland_76> All thanks to you

10:12:31 <crushedmarigolds> Happy I could help in any way I could

10:12:48 <agnes_in_wonderland_76> I know I already said this, but you really did change my life

10:12:58 <crushedmarigolds> I know

10:13:04 <agnes_in_wonderland_76> You really didn't have to do that

10:13:10 <crushedmarigolds> I wanted to

10:13:22 <crushedmarigolds> [omitted]

10:13:30 <agnes_in_wonderland_76> What are you doing right now?

10:13:42 <crushedmarigolds> Eating dinner, playing solitaire on the computer

10:13:51 <agnes_in_wonderland_76> Eating dinner this late?

10:14:02 <crushedmarigolds> Couldn't help it. I was busy all day

10:14:17 <crushedmarigolds> What are you doing?

10:14:29 <agnes_in_wonderland_76> Drinking a cup of tea, going to bed soon

10:14:42 <crushedmarigolds> Same. I can't stay on long. I have to get up early tomorrow

10:14:58 <agnes_in_wonderland_76> I wish you didn't have to

10:15:09 <crushedmarigolds> Me too. It's for work. Have to commute into the office

10:15:27 <agnes_in_wonderland_76> Will you be on tomorrow night?

10:15:36 <crushedmarigolds> Definitely

10:15:49 <agnes_in_wonderland_76> Good

10:16:01 <crushedmarigolds> Will you make me a promise?

10:16:11 <agnes_in_wonderland_76> Anything

10:16:28 <crushedmarigolds> Don't sell the apple peeler. Keep it for your grandmother

10:16:39 <agnes_in_wonderland_76> OK. I will

10:16:52 <crushedmarigolds> We'll talk tomorrow?

10:17:01 <agnes_in_wonderland_76> Yeah, we'll talk tomorrow

10:17:08 <crushedmarigolds> Talk to you then

10:17:14 <agnes_in_wonderland_76> Talk to you

[<crushedmarigolds> has left the chat]
[<agnes_in_wonderland_76> has left the chat]

PART
TWO

WHAT HAVE YOU DONE TODAY TO
DESERVE YOUR EYES?

EMAIL FROM AGNES PETRELLA

Date: 06/03/2000
Time: 8:08 a.m.
From: Agnes Petrella <agnes_in_wonderland_76@[omitted].com>
To: Zoe Cross <crushedmarigolds@[omitted].com>
Subject: Thinking of you

I know you're probably busy at work, but I wanted to send you a quick note and let you know that you've been on my mind all morning.

Is that weird?

I hope it's not weird.

I once read somewhere that if your mind continuously returns to the same person over and over again, it means that they're thinking of you as well.

I hope that's true.

I'd be absolutely devastated to know it was a lie conjured by somebody who simply had too much time on their hands.

Of course, I'm certain you're busy. You probably don't have the luxury of endless free time to think. It's not that I have the luxury of endless time on my hands either. But I can't seem to compel my brain to think of anything other than you and your kindness.

Another user on that QueerList website reached out to me this morning and inquired if the apple peeler was for sale. You can imagine my surprise when I received the email. I thought I had taken the post down. I suppose in my excitement yesterday, the thought completely slipped my mind.

You'll be happy to know I've since taken down the listing from the website. The apple peeler is safe in its decorative place, pinned to my kitchen wall. In fact, I'm staring at it right now as I type this email.

I hope we have the chance to talk again later tonight. I like talking to you.

I feel more like myself when I talk to you. I don't quite know what it is.

Until then,
Agnes

EMAIL FROM ZOE CROSS

Date: 06/03/2000

Time: 1:07 p.m.

From: Zoe Cross <crushedmarigolds@[omitted].com>

To: Agnes Petrella <agnes_in_wonderland_76@[omitted].com>

Subject: Re: Thinking of you

Agnes,

This will have to be a quick response as I'm currently swamped with work. But I wanted to take a moment and thank you for your email.

I'm delighted to hear you've removed your posting from the website and that the apple peeler is safe under your care. Well done. I wouldn't dream of having it any other way.

Unfortunately, I have plans for later this evening, so I won't be online much. I can certainly try to drop by around eleven o'clock or so if you'll still be awake.

I hope you will.

I look forward to it.

Zoe

INSTANT MESSAGING CONVERSATION BETWEEN AGNES AND ZOE

06/03/2000

[<crushedmarigolds> has entered the chat]

[<agnes_in_wonderland_76> has entered the chat]

11:04:05 <crushedmarigolds> Hey. You're still up

11:04:09 <crushedmarigolds> I'm glad

11:04:19 <agnes_in_wonderland_76> Can't stay long

11:04:28 <crushedmarigolds> I get it. It's late

11:04:39 <agnes_in_wonderland_76> Did you have fun?

11:04:44 <crushedmarigolds> Fun?

11:04:57 <agnes_in_wonderland_76> Wherever you were

11:05:09 <crushedmarigolds> I guess

11:05:18 <agnes_in_wonderland_76> Were you with someone else?

11:05:26 <crushedmarigolds> Someone else?

11:05:35 <agnes_in_wonderland_76> I know it's none of my business

11:05:47 <agnes_in_wonderland_76> Are you seeing someone?

11:05:52 <crushedmarigolds> I was

11:05:58 <crushedmarigolds> Not anymore

11:06:08 <agnes_in_wonderland_76> Because something happened

11:06:12 <crushedmarigolds> Yes

11:06:19 <crushedmarigolds> Well, no

11:06:29 <agnes_in_wonderland_76> You can tell me

11:06:36 <crushedmarigolds> Because we were living past the expiration date

11:06:46 <agnes_in_wonderland_76> Were you with them tonight?

11:06:51 <crushedmarigolds> We ended it tonight

11:07:00 <agnes_in_wonderland_76> So… you were with her

11:07:06 <crushedmarigolds> Yeah

11:07:14 <crushedmarigolds> I didn't want to tell you

11:07:20 <agnes_in_wonderland_76> Why?

11:07:27 <crushedmarigolds> Thought it might spoil what we have

11:07:39 <agnes_in_wonderland_76> Is she there right now?

11:07:46 <crushedmarigolds> No. She left

11:07:54 <crushedmarigolds> Gave me back her set of keys, too

11:08:01 <agnes_in_wonderland_76> Are you happy?

11:08:09 <crushedmarigolds> I will be someday

11:08:16 <agnes_in_wonderland_76> What are you doing right now?

11:08:25 <crushedmarigolds> Watching TV, eating some cereal

11:08:36 <agnes_in_wonderland_76> What are you watching?

11:08:42 <crushedmarigolds> Some travel program about Thailand

11:08:51 <crushedmarigolds> Did you know there's a place you can go to experience your own burial?

11:08:59 <crushedmarigolds> It's like a ritualized form of "pretend death"

11:09:09 <crushedmarigolds> You write your own eulogy, you're attended by a crowd of mourners

11:09:18 <crushedmarigolds> Then, you're interred in the earth for thirty minutes before you're exhumed

11:09:26 <agnes_in_wonderland_76> That's crazy

11:09:33 <crushedmarigolds> They give you an oxygen tank just in case, but I can't imagine doing it

11:09:39 <agnes_in_wonderland_76> Me neither

11:09:45 <crushedmarigolds> My father used to have a saying when I was really little…

11:09:52 <crushedmarigolds> At the end of each day, he used to ask me, "What have you done today to deserve your eyes?"

11:10:01 <crushedmarigolds> It took me years to understand what he actually meant

11:10:08 <crushedmarigolds> Our eyesight—among other things—is a gift that we take for granted

11:10:14 <crushedmarigolds> Right?

11:10:19 <agnes_in_wonderland_76> I suppose I haven't given it much thought

11:10:22 <crushedmarigolds> Exactly

11:10:29 <crushedmarigolds> It's not something we always think about until we lose it

11:10:38 <crushedmarigolds> We don't covet our hands until we lose a finger

11:10:43 <crushedmarigolds> We don't praise our hearing until we lose an ear

11:10:52 <crushedmarigolds> What have you done today to deserve your eyes?

11:11:04 <agnes_in_wonderland_76> You're asking me?

11:11:10 <crushedmarigolds> You can't answer, can you?

11:11:19 <agnes_in_wonderland_76> I guess I've never really thought about it

11:11:28 <crushedmarigolds> I'm going to hold you accountable from now on

11:11:37 <agnes_in_wonderland_76> Are you?

11:11:43 <crushedmarigolds> I'm going to check in each day and make certain you've done at least one thing to "deserve your eyes"

11:11:51 <crushedmarigolds> I'm not kidding

11:11:59 <agnes_in_wonderland_76> I believe you

11:12:07 <crushedmarigolds> I'm going to ask you start tomorrow

11:12:13 <agnes_in_wonderland_76> And how should I do that?

11:12:20 <crushedmarigolds> Where do you work?

11:12:29 <agnes_in_wonderland_76> [omitted]

11:12:36 <crushedmarigolds> It's an office building?

11:12:41 <agnes_in_wonderland_76> Yes. I'm one of the receptionists

11:12:50 <crushedmarigolds> You're going to make a statement

11:12:58 <agnes_in_wonderland_76> What kind of statement?

11:13:04 <crushedmarigolds> You're going to go out this weekend and buy a brand-new red dress

11:13:15 <crushedmarigolds> You're going to clip the tags so that you can't return it and you're going to wear it to work

11:13:21 <agnes_in_wonderland_76> A red dress at work? I'll be drawn and quartered

11:13:30 <crushedmarigolds> That's not all. You're going to buy a tube of blood red lipstick and wear it with your new dress

11:13:39 <agnes_in_wonderland_76> You must be out of your mind

11:13:47 <crushedmarigolds> I want you to take a picture of yourself in the employee bathroom and send it to me as proof

11:13:54 <agnes_in_wonderland_76> You've got to be joking

11:14:03 <crushedmarigolds> I'll be expecting the proof from you

11:14:12 <crushedmarigolds> I'll be expecting proof that you deserve your eyes

11:14:19 <crushedmarigolds> Do we have a deal?

11:14:29 <agnes_in_wonderland_76> I guess so

11:14:38 <crushedmarigolds> Perfect

11:14:45 <agnes_in_wonderland_76> I can't believe I'm doing this

11:14:57 <crushedmarigolds> Pick the brightest, bloodiest red you can find

11:15:06 <crushedmarigolds> I'll talk to you tomorrow?

11:15:10 <agnes_in_wonderland_76> Yes. Talk to you tomorrow

[<crushedmarigolds> has left the chat]
[<agnes_in_wonderland_76> has left the chat]

EMAIL FROM AGNES PETRELLA

Date: 06/05/2000
Time: 7:12 p.m.
From: Agnes Petrella <agnes_in_wonderland_76@[omitted].com>
To: Zoe Cross <crushedmarigolds@[omitted].com>
Subject: The Red Dress
[Picture attached] [Omitted]

You'll be delighted to know that today I did the unthinkable.

I went to the department store during my lunch break and asked one of the sales associates where I could find the brightest, most garish red dress they had in stock. I was whisked away to the rear of the store by a short old woman who smelled of jasmine and pipe tobacco.

And there it was.

As decadently red as a severed artery in full bloom.

The old woman escorted me to the fitting room, and I slipped the dress on as if it were a second layer of skin. I couldn't imagine taking it off. It felt so irresistibly perfect, as if it were the tightening embrace of a long lost loved one— someone I had met in a former life and was reunited with after centuries spent pining for their homecoming.

"Would you like to wear it out of the store?" the saleswoman asked me.

I caught my reflection in the paneled mirror at the end of the dressing room's corridor, and I do a double take because the girl I see standing there cannot possibly be me. She's smiling. She doesn't hide her lips behind trembling fingers as if her mouth were an untreated wound.

So, I passed my credit card to the saleswoman, and she handed me a paper bag containing a neatly folded pile of my old clothes—the snakeskin I had molted and shed so effortlessly. And to think I could have done it this whole time. I cursed myself for being so contented, being so comfortable to remain as I once was—an insect burdened with a shell far too big for the smallness of their size.

But, before I left the store, I circled the makeup counter and peered through the collection of lipstick arranged in the case as if they were fine Parisian delicacies. I finally found the color I was looking for—"Red Velvet." I asked the saleswoman for the last tube of lipstick and she passed the small capsule to me. Angling the mirror on the counter toward me, I twisted the lipstick until it sprouted open and then smeared it across my lips until they were the dark color of a beetroot.

I returned to work and that's when I noticed that when you change, the people around you start to change as well. The arched eyebrows. The voices thinning to mere whispers. The spines straightening, faces blanching, as if I were brandishing a small weapon when I passed them. I suppose I was—the redness sprawling from every inch of my body as if I were blanketed with a rare tropical flower, a carnivorous plant with a decidedly avid appetite.

It wasn't long before one of the other secretaries—a woman I absolutely loathe with a short blonde pixie haircut—approached me at my desk and explained how my superior wanted to see me in her office at once.

So, I crept into her office and found her sitting there at her desk, sipping a cup of tea and waiting for me.

"Sit down, Agnes," she said, resting her cup of tea on a small saucer beside her pile of papers.

God, this can't be good, I thought to myself. Although I had expected attention for my new wardrobe choices, I hardly expected it would land me in my boss's office.

"We've had some… complaints regarding your new attire," she explained. "Some of the other employees have felt your colors are a bit… distracting."

Normally, I would have retreated—curled up inside myself, coiled like a mamba in some secret part of myself where not even shame or guilt can follow.

But, much to my surprise, I didn't.

I found myself stretching out, as if pleased to show her how wicked I can be—as if I were that very same carnivorous plant they thought of me, the very same monster they had already named me.

"We're going to ask you take the rest of the day off," she told me.

So, I packed my things and left the office for the day. When I walked, it felt as if a thick red weed sprouted from each of my footprints—a trail for anyone daring enough to follow.

I think I've earned my eyes for another day. Don't you?

Agnes

EMAIL FROM ZOE CROSS

Date: 06/05/2000
Time: 8:41 p.m.
From: Zoe Cross <crushedmarigolds@[omitted].com>
To: Agnes Petrella <agnes_in_wonderland_76@[omitted].com>
Subject: Re: The Red Dress

Agnes,

I am so delighted to hear you've reclaimed your power and that you're making colossal strides toward the ownership of your true identity—a fearless young woman. I knew that pushing you would result in something truly glorious, but I never expected you to present yourself with such dedication and resilience.

I'm truly impressed.

I knew defying the conventions of your place of employment's dress code would be exactly the thing you needed to recognize your true worth as a person. I only wish I could have been there to witness the carnage unfold.

I look forward to discussing more tonight on Instant Messenger. I should be on around ten-thirty, if you can make it.

I hope this isn't too forward. (But, then again, I feel as though we have no more boundaries between us.) If you'd truly like to make a bold statement and embrace your new identity, go the rest of the week without wearing any underwear.

Talk to you tonight,
Zoe

INSTANT MESSAGING CONVERSATION
BETWEEN AGNES AND ZOE

06/05/2000
[<crushedmarigolds> has entered the chat]
[<agnes_in_wonderland_76> has entered the chat]

10:34:02 <crushedmarigolds> Hey

10:34:09 <crushedmarigolds> How does the snake feel in her new skin?

10:34:18 <agnes_in_wonderland_76> I feel like I could burst into flames

10:34:28 <agnes_in_wonderland_76> I've never felt this way before

10:34:37 <crushedmarigolds> Didn't take much

10:34:49 <agnes_in_wonderland_76> I could've never done this without you

10:34:59 <crushedmarigolds> We're all capable of change. Sometimes it hurts

10:35:07 <agnes_in_wonderland_76> You know what I feel like?

10:35:16 <agnes_in_wonderland_76> I feel like a new constellation, scabbed in glittering black

10:35:20 <agnes_in_wonderland_76> A smear across the universe

10:35:28 <crushedmarigolds> Wait for the asteroid to come

10:35:40 <agnes_in_wonderland_76> No. I feel like some shapeless cosmic belt, as if the hand of some invisible deity were cradling me in his arms

10:35:49 <agnes_in_wonderland_76> [omitted]

10:35:57 <crushedmarigolds> You know, I wasn't joking about the underwear...

10:36:05 <agnes_in_wonderland_76> Yeah?

10:36:09 <crushedmarigolds> Yeah...

10:36:17 <agnes_in_wonderland_76> I've been thinking about it

10:36:29 <crushedmarigolds> And?

10:36:41 <agnes_in_wonderland_76> Do you like thinking about me not wearing any underwear?

10:36:48 <crushedmarigolds> It's a thought I don't mind

10:36:59 <agnes_in_wonderland_76> Maybe you'd like to tell me what else is on your mind?

10:37:08 <crushedmarigolds> Can't

10:37:13 <agnes_in_wonderland_76> Why not?

10:37:19 <crushedmarigolds> It would scare you

10:37:27 <agnes_in_wonderland_76> It wouldn't

10:37:42 <crushedmarigolds> My thoughts scare me sometimes

10:37:49 <agnes_in_wonderland_76> Whatever you're thinking, I probably want it

10:37:58 <crushedmarigolds> Do you?

10:38:06 <agnes_in_wonderland_76> Yeah

10:38:18 <crushedmarigolds> You'd like me to tie your hands

with rope above your head and use a leather crop to blacken both of your ass cheeks?

10:38:27 <agnes_in_wonderland_76> Yes

10:38:35 <crushedmarigolds> How about I open you up with my fingers until they slide in deep inside, soft gurgling noises clogged in the pit of your throat?

10:38:43 <agnes_in_wonderland_76> Yeah. Don't stop, baby

10:38:49 <crushedmarigolds> You going to open up for Mommy?

10:38:59 <crushedmarigolds> I push in further and you're fully open for me

10:39:08 <agnes_in_wonderland_76> It's all for you, Mommy

10:39:12 <agnes_in_wonderland_76> I'm touching myself right now

10:39:19 <agnes_in_wonderland_76> Are you?

10:39:30 <agnes_in_wonderland_76> Why did you stop?

10:39:51 <crushedmarigolds> Don't want to scare you away

10:40:01 <agnes_in_wonderland_76> You're not going to scare me, I promise

10:40:09 <crushedmarigolds> You're going to ask what I want

10:40:18 <agnes_in_wonderland_76> What's the matter with that?

10:40:29 <crushedmarigolds> The problem is I know exactly what I want, and it's something no woman could ever give me

10:40:38 <agnes_in_wonderland_76> I could try

10:40:43 <crushedmarigolds> No

10:40:49 <agnes_in_wonderland_76> You've done so much for me. I'm happy to

10:40:57 <agnes_in_wonderland_76> What is it?

10:41:05 <crushedmarigolds> I can't talk right now

10:41:13 <agnes_in_wonderland_76> Is someone there with you?

10:41:22 <crushedmarigolds> No. Nobody's here

10:41:28 <crushedmarigolds> I have to go

10:41:35 <crushedmarigolds> I'll talk to you later?

10:41:44 <agnes_in_wonderland_76> Yeah. I guess I'll talk to you later

[<crushedmarigolds> has left the chat]
[<agnes_in_wonderland_76> has left the chat]

INSTANT MESSAGING CONVERSATION BETWEEN AGNES AND ZOE

06/06/2000

[<crushedmarigolds> has entered the chat]

[<agnes_in_wonderland_76> has entered the chat]

1:39:09 <agnes_in_wonderland_76> You came back

1:39:14 <crushedmarigolds> Have you been waiting this whole time?

1:39:25 <agnes_in_wonderland_76> I couldn't sleep

1:39:33 <agnes_in_wonderland_76> I had hoped you'd come back

1:39:46 <agnes_in_wonderland_76> Why did you leave?

1:39:54 <crushedmarigolds> I was scared

1:39:55 <agnes_in_wonderland_76> Scared of what?

1:40:03 <crushedmarigolds> Losing you

1:40:12 <agnes_in_wonderland_76> Why would you lose me?

1:40:20 <crushedmarigolds> Because I thought about telling you what I really wanted

1:40:29 <agnes_in_wonderland_76> I want you to tell me. I need you to tell me

1:40:46 <crushedmarigolds> You won't be scared?

1:40:57 <agnes_in_wonderland_76> You could never scare me

1:41:05 <crushedmarigolds> I want a woman to belong to me

1:41:13 <agnes_in_wonderland_76> I want that, too

1:41:22 <crushedmarigolds> No, you don't get it

1:41:34 <agnes_in_wonderland_76> I'm trying. Just help me out

1:41:39 <crushedmarigolds> I want somebody I can take care of—in every possible way

1:41:44 <agnes_in_wonderland_76> Yes

1:41:49 <crushedmarigolds> Somebody who answers only to me, as if I were the hand of God that feeds them

1:42:03 <crushedmarigolds> Somebody who would be willing to give up their freedom so that I could command them

1:42:12 <crushedmarigolds> I would have access to their email, their bank account—every little thing that makes up a fully formed person

1:42:19 <crushedmarigolds> They would belong to me and, in return, I would take care of them the way a mother nurtures a child

1:42:28 <crushedmarigolds> They would never work another day in their life, unless they wanted to

1:42:39 <crushedmarigolds> I would do everything in my power to protect them, to care for them—as long as they willingly gave themselves to me

1:42:54 <crushedmarigolds> Are you still there?

1:43:01 <agnes_in_wonderland_76> I'm here

1:43:09 <crushedmarigolds> Are you scared?

1:43:17 <agnes_in_wonderland_76> No

1:43:26 <crushedmarigolds> You asked what I wanted

1:43:33 <agnes_in_wonderland_76> Yes, I wanted to know

1:43:40 <crushedmarigolds> I understand if you'd rather keep your distance for awhile

1:43:49 <agnes_in_wonderland_76> I'll do it

1:43:58 <crushedmarigolds> What?

1:44:06 <agnes_in_wonderland_76> I would give myself entirely to you

1:44:17 <agnes_in_wonderland_76> After everything you've done for me

1:44:27 <crushedmarigolds> You're serious?

1:44:39 <agnes_in_wonderland_76> I told you I wanted to repay you for your kindness

1:44:44 <crushedmarigolds> No

1:44:52 <agnes_in_wonderland_76> What do you mean, "no?"

1:45:03 <crushedmarigolds> I want you to say "yes" because it's something you want, yearn for. Not because it's a debt you feel you need to repay

1:45:10 <agnes_in_wonderland_76> It's something I want, believe me

1:45:19 <agnes_in_wonderland_76> If you promise to take care of me

1:45:28 <crushedmarigolds> I would

1:45:37 <agnes_in_wonderland_76> Then, it's something I want

1:45:49 <crushedmarigolds> You're sure you're willing to do this?

1:45:59 <agnes_in_wonderland_76> I would do anything for you

1:46:04 <crushedmarigolds> Yes

1:46:09 <agnes_in_wonderland_76> I'm serious

1:46:18 <crushedmarigolds> If you're serious, I'll draw up
   a contract

1:46:22 <agnes_in_wonderland_76> Fancy

1:46:29 <crushedmarigolds> I'll send it over in a day or two

1:46:38 <agnes_in_wonderland_76> I'll be waiting for it

1:46:44 <crushedmarigolds> Talk soon?

1:46:50 <agnes_in_wonderland_76> Yeah, talk soon

[<crushedmarigolds> has left the chat]

[<agnes_in_wonderland_76> has left the chat]

EMAIL FROM ZOE CROSS

[The following is an email sent from Zoe Cross's email account to Agnes Petrella's where she tortuously details the intricacies of their proposed Master/Slave relationship. As with most other sections of text in this publication, certain areas of writing have been censored or redacted under the supervision of the Henley's Edge Police Department. These areas have been written as [omitted].]

Date: 06/07/2000

Time: 10:06 a.m.

From: Zoe Cross <crushedmarigolds@[omitted].com>

To: Agnes Petrella <agnes_in_wonderland_76@[omitted].com>

Subject: Contract Agreement

CONTRACT AGREEMENT

between

<u>Zoe Cross</u>

and

<u>Agnes Petrella</u>

<u>Zoe Cross</u>, hereinafter referred to as "Sponsor," hereby binds this contract with <u>Agnes Petrella</u>, hereinafter referred to as

"Drudge," in this Contract of Sponsorship. Said contract refers to total dominance and control of Owner in this relationship with said "Drudge" in regard to the stipulations contained herein. It is to be noted that the official agreement was reached on the day of June 7th, 2000. This contract is to be a written declaration of this fact.

This contract is in no way legally binding in a court of law but is meant as an aid to better understanding of the needs, duties, and responsibilities of the Sponsor and the Drudge. Both the Sponsor and Drudge agree upon the details of this relationship, with both parties accepting and understanding the consequences of such.

[Omitted]

PURPOSE
The purpose of this instrument is to:
- State the full mutual consent of the above mentioned in regard to this relationship
- Explain the responsibilities and duties of both Sponsor and Drudge
- Explain the use of punishment
- Define all set rules and possible future rules

This contract is written to make clear the expectations of Sponsor and the consequences for failure to live up to this agreement.

———

The said parties, for the consideration hereinafter mentioned, hereby agree to the following:

1. The Drudge agrees to obey to the best of her ability, and to devote herself entirely to the pleasures and desires of the Sponsor. The Drudge also renounces all rights to her own pleasure, comfort, or gratification except insofar as permitted by the Sponsor.

2. The Drudge agrees to hand over the password and all subsequent details of her bank account information to the Sponsor so that the Sponsor is in full control of her accounts. The Drudge agrees to never question the Sponsor with regard to finances and fully understands that the Sponsor's full possession of her account is for her physical and mental well-being.

3. The Drudge will sleep in the nude with the air conditioning on full blast, even in winter months. This is intended to show servitude to the Sponsor and is a means by which the Drudge can make a small sacrifice in order to exhibit an unparalleled level of loyalty.

4. The Drudge will only consume food at the following times: 10 a.m., 1 p.m., and 6 p.m. This strict regimen of feeding will not only improve digestion but will keep the Drudge balanced and in good faith with the Sponsor.

5. The Drudge will confer with the Sponsor before making any large purchases as the Sponsor holds the account information for the Drudge.

6. The Sponsor accepts full responsibility for the Drudge. This includes but is not limited to: the Drudge's survival,

health, physical well-being, and mental well-being. The Drudge accepts full responsibility for informing the Sponsor of any real or perceived dangers or safety concerns, but also agrees that the Sponsor's decision will be final regarding these issues.

7. The Drudge agrees and understands that any infractions of this contract, or any act the Drudge commits which displeases the Sponsor, will result in punishment.

8. This agreement may not be assigned by either party to any third party.

9. This agreement may be amended in writing at the Sponsor's behest and will require compliance from both parties.

[Omitted]

This contract is valid from the day the Drudge replies to this email with "Accepted, understood, and agreed to" and is effective for all time unless terminated by the Sponsor.

EMAIL FROM AGNES PETRELLA

Date: 06/07/2000

Time: 12:05 p.m.

From: Agnes Petrella <agnes_in_wonderland_76@[omitted].com>

To: Zoe Cross <crushedmarigolds@[omitted].com>

Subject: Re: Contract Agreement

Accepted, understood, and agreed to.

Signed,
Agnes Petrella

PART THREE

A SALAMANDER FROM THE PARK

EMAIL FROM ZOE CROSS

Date: 06/08/2000
Time: 6:49 a.m.
From: Zoe Cross <crushedmarigolds@[omitted].com>
To: Agnes Petrella <agnes_in_wonderland_76@[omitted].com>
Subject: A Drudge's Duties

Good morning, Drudge,

I trust you slept well.

I imagine you're getting ready to leave for work, and that's precisely why I'm emailing you.

I have another task for you. Something that will undoubtedly make you uncomfortable. Then again, aren't those the moments when we change the most—when we're uncomfortable?

I'd like you to go into the communal bathroom at work and leave your undergarments in the stall for someone to find. Perhaps a pair embellished with lace, or maybe a pair you've yet to wash.

Regardless of the pair you choose, I want the undergarment deserted in a conspicuous place—where someone can and will find it.

I trust you will complete this task in as expeditious a manner as possible and will reply to this message with "Done" when you have properly executed the assignment.

What have you done today to deserve your eyes?

Yours,
Sponsor

EMAIL FROM AGNES PETRELLA

Date: 06/08/2000
Time: 9:09 a.m.
From: Agnes Petrella <agnes_in_wonderland_76@[omitted].com>
To: Zoe Cross <crushedmarigolds@[omitted].com>
Subject: Re: A Drudge's Duties

Done.

   Signed,
   Agnes Petrella

EMAIL FROM AGNES PETRELLA

Date: 06/08/2000

Time: 2:17 p.m.

From: Agnes Petrella <agnes_in_wonderland_76@[omitted].com>

To: Zoe Cross <crushedmarigolds@[omitted].com>

Subject: Re: A Drudge's Duties

Well, it finally happened.

I was asked to leave today. Only this time, for good.

I crept into the ladies' washroom when I was certain it was empty, skirted into one of the empty stalls, and slid off the pair of underwear I wore to work today. It was a dark cherry color, the edges frilled with lace as finely woven as a spider's web.

When I had fully removed the underwear, wrenching it off from around my shoes, I wrapped the garment around the toilet seat's handlebar. I stepped back, admiring the finesse of my craftsmanship. The underwear dangled there obscenely as if it were human viscera on display—a juiceless organ or a dried-out intestine to be marveled at.

After I was satisfied with my work, I crawled out of the empty stall. But just as I was leaving, one of the other secretaries greeted me at the washroom door. She made a friendly comment, excusing herself as she almost bumped into me. Then, I watched her eyes drift to the undergarments hanging from the handlebar in the empty stall.

She looked at me strangely, as if searching me for an explanation. When she could find none, she made her way into one of the other stalls and shut the door.

I sneaked back to my desk and waited for the moment when it would happen—the moment when I would be once again asked to visit my superior's office. Only this time, I decided I would accept my fate with the same dignity of a virgin martyr being led to public execution.

Finally, the time came.

"She'd like to see you in her office," one of the other younger secretaries told me while keeping their distance, as if I carried some infectious disease and they might be dismissed as well if they came too close to me.

The meeting was brief. Just as I had expected. A simple, "You're dismissed," and a few papers to sign.

I didn't feel anything when I was asked to pack my things. I thought I might feel a pinch in the center of my chest, a faucet leaking behind my eyes. But no. Nothing.

It's not that I felt empty. I think all of us feel empty most of the time and we merely pretend to fill the vacuum with laughter, crying, apologies—anything to make us feel human.

I think I felt like what an astronaut feels like when they hurtle toward earth in a tiny prison chamber, flames eating away at their vessel as they enter our atmosphere.

There's a reason objects burn up when they fall to earth like gruesome angels—a reason other than the obvious one. Asteroids the size of armored cars narrow to mere pebbles in a matter of seconds. It's because the planet is a carnivore and just wants to be fed. People want that as well. People like to eat other people.

I spent so many years forgetting I had teeth, too.

So, I packed my things up and hurried out of the office, swiping the underwear from the washroom stall before I forgot. I stepped out onto the street, daylight running its fingers through my hair as if it were a fire. That's when I thought of you.

I know you'll take care of me.

You won't eat me. No matter how much you enjoy the way I taste.

EMAIL FROM ZOE CROSS

Date: 06/08/2000

Time: 4:13 p.m.

From: Zoe Cross <crushedmarigolds@[omitted].com>

To: Agnes Petrella <agnes_in_wonderland_76@[omitted].com>

Subject: Re: A Drudge's Duties

Drudge,

I'm devastated to learn of your recent dismissal. But I'm delighted to know you don't view this slight impediment as a major setback.

In truth, I was considering reaching out to you and explaining that you no longer need to work when you're under my care. I assured you that I will take care of you, and I certainly do not intend to neglect my side of our agreement.

We can discuss this further tonight on Instant Messenger. I'll be on at ten o'clock. I expect to see you there.

Signed,
Sponsor

INSTANT MESSAGING CONVERSATION BETWEEN AGNES AND ZOE

06/08/2000
[<crushedmarigolds> has entered the chat]
[<agnes_in_wonderland_76> has entered the chat]

10:01:04 <agnes_in_wonderland_76> Hi

10:01:08 <crushedmarigolds> You're late

10:01:14 <agnes_in_wonderland_76> I'm sorry

10:01:20 <crushedmarigolds> Sorry what?

10:01:31 <agnes_in_wonderland_76> Sorry, Sponsor

10:01:43 <crushedmarigolds> That's a good Drudge

10:01:52 <crushedmarigolds> You understand the penance for being late?

10:02:03 <agnes_in_wonderland_76> Yes, Sponsor

10:02:14 <crushedmarigolds> You're to hold your breath for a minute

10:02:22 <agnes_in_wonderland_76> Yes, Sponsor

10:02:34 <crushedmarigolds> Deep breath

10:02:39 <crushedmarigolds> Starting now

10:02:45 <crushedmarigolds> Don't breathe

10:02:52 <crushedmarigolds> Not yet

10:03:05 <crushedmarigolds> Keep it held

10:03:14 <crushedmarigolds> Not done yet

10:03:22 <crushedmarigolds> Almost there

10:03:29 <crushedmarigolds> Almost

10:03:35 <crushedmarigolds> Now

10:03:39 <crushedmarigolds> Breathe

10:03:49 <crushedmarigolds> What do you say?

10:03:55 <agnes_in_wonderland_76> Thank you, Sponsor

10:04:07 <crushedmarigolds> That's a good girl

10:04:15 <crushedmarigolds> Now, the matter of your allowance...

10:04:22 <agnes_in_wonderland_76> Allowance?

10:04:31 <crushedmarigolds> Don't you think that's fair?

10:04:44 <agnes_in_wonderland_76> Yes. I guess so...

10:04:50 <agnes_in_wonderland_76> That's very generous of you

10:05:01 <crushedmarigolds> I'll deposit fifteen hundred dollars in your account on the first of every month

10:05:11 <agnes_in_wonderland_76> Fifteen hundred?!!

10:05:22 <crushedmarigolds> A fair amount?

10:05:29 <agnes_in_wonderland_76> I would say so

10:05:33 <agnes_in_wonderland_76> It's too generous

10:05:41 <crushedmarigolds> You know Mommy wants to take care of her girl

10:05:55 <agnes_in_wonderland_76> Yes. I know

10:06:03 <crushedmarigolds> Is there anything you want?

10:06:11 <agnes_in_wonderland_76> Anything I want?

10:06:19 <crushedmarigolds> If you could have anything

10:06:29 <crushedmarigolds> Name it

10:06:38 <agnes_in_wonderland_76> I want to see you in person

10:06:44 <agnes_in_wonderland_76> I want to be able to touch you

10:06:55 <agnes_in_wonderland_76> To know you're real

10:07:04 <crushedmarigolds> Aren't I real enough for you already?

10:07:12 <agnes_in_wonderland_76> You're just a blinking cursor to me right now

10:07:20 <agnes_in_wonderland_76> I want to know you're real

10:07:31 <agnes_in_wonderland_76> To feel your blood pumping, the heartbeat in your hands

10:07:40 <crushedmarigolds> I've already done so much to prove to you I'm real

10:07:51 <agnes_in_wonderland_76> I suppose I just can't believe a person as good as you exists

10:08:03 <agnes_in_wonderland_76> Don't you want us to be together?

10:08:10 <crushedmarigolds> Of course I do

10:08:21 <crushedmarigolds> How could you ask me that?

10:08:30 <agnes_in_wonderland_76> Then, why can't we?

10:08:44 <crushedmarigolds> It's not that I don't want to

10:08:52 <crushedmarigolds> We're not ready yet

10:09:01 <agnes_in_wonderland_76> Will we be?

10:09:09 <crushedmarigolds> Someday

10:09:17 <crushedmarigolds> Just not today

10:09:24 <agnes_in_wonderland_76> You asked me if there's something I want

10:09:29 <crushedmarigolds> Yes

10:09:34 <agnes_in_wonderland_76> More than anything in the world

10:09:43 <crushedmarigolds> Tell me

10:09:55 <agnes_in_wonderland_76> I want a baby

10:10:02 <crushedmarigolds> Yes

10:10:15 <agnes_in_wonderland_76> I want life to carry inside me

10:10:25 <agnes_in_wonderland_76> That's what I've wanted more than anything else

10:10:33 <agnes_in_wonderland_76> To be a mother

10:10:56 <agnes_in_wonderland_76> You still there?

10:11:03 <crushedmarigolds> I wish I could give you that

10:11:09 <crushedmarigolds> I would if I could

10:11:17 <agnes_in_wonderland_76> I know you would

10:11:28 <crushedmarigolds> I can't stay

10:11:37 <agnes_in_wonderland_76> You have to leave already?

10:11:48 <crushedmarigolds> We'll talk tomorrow?

10:11:55 <agnes_in_wonderland_76> Always

[<crushedmarigolds> has left the chat]

[<agnes_in_wonderland_76> has left the chat]

EMAIL FROM ZOE CROSS

Date: 06/10/2000

Time: 2:04 a.m.

From: Zoe Cross <crushedmarigolds@[omitted].com>

To: Agnes Petrella <agnes_in_wonderland_76@[omitted].com>

Subject: A Salamander from the Park

I thought of something before going to bed tonight. I've been thinking a lot about what you said—how you want to carry life, how you want something to care for.

I think there's a way for us both to get what we want.

I want you to visit a park near your apartment. I checked on the map, and I see that there's a place called White Memorial not far from where you live.

I want you to go there and comb the grounds for a salamander.

A wet, oily little thing—probably could contentedly fit inside the palm of your hand.

You can usually find them in moist areas. They prefer marshlands—freshwater creeks or brooks. I've read they typically hide under rocks, their little bodies seeking out damp, cool places.

I want you to take the salamander from where you find it

and stuff it inside your pocket. Keep it tucked there so that it's comfortable. I want you to carry it with you all day. No matter where you go. If it suffocates in there, I want you to return to the park and find another one.

I want you to do this all day until sunset.

Then, when twilight devours color from the sky, I want you to take the salamander to a place outdoors where nobody can find you. I want you to find a large rock and smash it against the small creature until it stops moving.

You probably didn't know the salamander is a symbol of rebirth in many cultures—a sign of change, transformation, and growth.

Don't you wish to be reborn too?

After all, what have you done today to deserve your eyes?

Signed,
Sponsor

EMAIL FROM AGNES PETRELLA

Date: 06/10/2000
Time: 8:37 a.m.
From: Agnes Petrella <agnes_in_wonderland_76@[omitted].com>
To: Zoe Cross <crushedmarigolds@[omitted].com>
Subject: Re: A Salamander from the Park

Sponsor,

I've read your email several times now and I'm uncertain where to begin.

You know I would never question you or do anything to challenge your judgment. But I don't think I could go through with it.

I could never hurt a living thing.

Will you please reconsider and give me another task?

I'll do anything else. I swear it.

Signed,
Drudge

EMAIL FROM ZOE CROSS

Date: 06/10/2000

Time: 9:49 a.m.

From: Zoe Cross <crushedmarigolds@[omitted].com>

To: Agnes Petrella <agnes_in_wonderland_76@[omitted].com>

Subject: Re: A Salamander from the Park

A Drudge does not question their Sponsor. A Drudge obeys no matter what.

EMAIL FROM AGNES PETRELLA

Date: 06/10/2000
Time: 10:11 p.m.
From: Agnes Petrella <agnes_in_wonderland_76@[omitted].com>
To: Zoe Cross <crushedmarigolds@[omitted].com>
Subject: Re: A Salamander from the Park

I did what you asked me to.

I didn't take pictures of any of it, so my account of everything will have to suffice.

I got in my car and took a drive out to the park this afternoon. The one you mentioned in your email. There was a huge iron gate that greeted me when I arrived, miniature stone gargoyles flanking either side that seemed to regard me as if incredulous, as if they were about to ask me what I was doing there. At the time, I remember thinking how wonderful it might be if one day we had a place with a gate guarded by little stone beasts with ferocious jaws—little creatures that would belong to us and no one else.

So, after I paid the attendant, I drove through the gate and began to meander down a narrow corridor lined with giant sycamores. I remember thinking, "What am I doing?"

"I shouldn't be here."

"I shouldn't be doing this."

"This is wrong."

But, with every barbed thought, I sensed my feet pushed down harder on the accelerator as if I were gleefully headed toward doom, as if I had caught a glimpse of Hell for the first time and needed to marvel further at its vast wealth of wonders.

I parked my car under a tree and headed for the pond I saw in the distance. There were a few children playing with their parents in the field beside the parking lot, but they didn't seem to notice me.

Creeping down the narrow causeway, I arrived at the pond. The water was still, lilies the size of dinner plates floating by. I started to skirt around the edges of the pond, my head craning beneath the underbrush beside the path. I located some small rocks on the water's shore, flipping them over and finding nothing.

Then, after an hour or so of searching, I noticed a small, dark shape stirring in the grass further up ahead near the water's edge. I looked closer and it was then I found what I was looking for—a salamander, the size of a housekey and practically just as flat. Its tail was slippery wet, and its skin glinted in the sunlight as I spooned it from the ground to hold in my hand.

There's something Godlike about holding something so small—something that solely depends on your kindness, your generosity. I had never thought about hurting something before. Until now. I imagined what it might feel like. I imagined closing my hand to make a fist until its tiny body was squished, its innards squeezed out like toothpaste from its mouth open in a muted scream.

Before I allowed myself to get too carried away with the thought, I shoved the little creature inside my pocket. I named him Albert and promised I would treat him with crickets if he behaved. He wouldn't know the difference if I didn't, and I knew he wouldn't call me a liar.

So, as promised, I carried him with me all day, my eyes glancing at my wristwatch every minute or so as if I were anticipating my own execution at twilight. Finally, the moment I had been dreading arrived—all light vacuumed from the sky.

So, I returned to the park after dusk and I took the little creature to a small grove of trees just beyond the parking lot. I sprawled him out along a moss-covered rock, and I searched for a rock nearby. When I finally located one—about the size of a bowling ball—I approached Albert with a wordless apology. He remained perfectly still, as if comfortable in my presence and foolishly thinking I would never do anything to harm him.

Before another moment of hesitation, I brought down the rock and slammed it against him. I heard a vulgar, wet thud. I looked down and saw the poor, pathetic creature— flattened—and crumpled like windblown paper against the rock's underside. After peeling his little body from the rock, he flopped to the ground and twitched gently before I saw his tiny legs stop from trembling.

The whole forest seemed to fall quiet, as if in mourning for the small creature.

So, I found a spot beneath a tree and dug a small hole in

the dirt. I ladled his little body from the ground and said a prayer before tossing him into the tiny pit I had opened.

I stood there at his grave for what felt like hours. Then, when darkness leached through the trees, I packed my things, headed for my car, and drove back home.

As I sit here at my computer, with dirt beneath my fingernails, I wonder why I did this, why I ever agreed to let you tell me what to do.

I never thought I would ever do something as monstrous, as wicked as this.

That poor creature didn't deserve to die, and I did it just to please you.

What else will I do to make you happy?

What else will I do before you finally take my eyes from me, as you've been promising?

You and I are better off without each other.

If we stay together, we'll only hurt one another.

I've been thinking about that a lot lately. Especially about a Sumatran short-eared rabbit. Have you ever seen one? It's a type of rabbit only found in Indonesia. Considered very rare. Endangered, in fact. They had one at the zoo I used to go to when I was in college. I used to skip my French class and instead take a walk to the zoo—stroll through the gardens, look at the orangutans and the lemurs, and the sloths and the pandas.

But I always found myself drawn to a small glass case framed on the pathway leading to the anteater exhibit. A small glass case with a female Sumatran short-eared rabbit inside. She'd squat in her little cage, her tiny hands cupping the bits of tropical fruit they'd give her. Her fur—warm chestnut with dark brown stripes. She was about as big as your hand. Maybe a little bit bigger.

I found out she was pregnant.

And the zookeepers were taking bets when she'd finally deliver the litter.

So, I kept checking back every day—ignoring my French homework and instead sprinting to the zoo to see if the rabbit had her babies yet.

And finally, one day, when I was there, she was lying on her side and it started to happen. Squeezing out of her was this tiny, pink clump of tissue—glistening wet. She labored for probably twenty minutes before the little thing pushed itself out of her, its limbs shiny and rubbery. And as it lay there, twitching in the agony of what it feels like to first become a living thing, she pressed her snout against it and inhaled its scent.

She did this a few times, pushing herself against the infant harder each time as if testing its comfort. And finally, as she started to give birth to the next baby, she wrapped her mouth around the rabbit she had just delivered and started devouring it.

I just stood there, watching helplessly as the mother rabbit ate her child—bits of tissue and blood smearing against her gnarled fur.

I didn't watch the rest of the carnage.

I walked back to my dorm, not remembering how I got there when I finally arrived. I went back to the zoo a month or so later and one of the zookeepers told me that the mother ate the other baby as well—not long after she ate the first one.

He said the baby rabbit was sick and wouldn't have survived even if they'd intervened in time. Said this happens all the time in the wild because a carcass will usually draw predators to the den. He said it was probably for the best.

Just like this decision is for the best.

This is where it stops.

I've made the decision not to go forward with our contract. I will not be answering any more of your emails, nor will I be financially engaging with you in any way.

I will be going to my bank tomorrow and wiring the money back into your account. I will also be closing my accounts and doing my banking elsewhere so that you no longer have access to my finances.

I'm petitioning you to please void our current contract as I refuse to move forward with any of your tasks.

I'm better off without you.

Signed,
Agnes

EMAIL FROM ZOE CROSS

Date: 06/10/2000
Time: 11:39 p.m.
From: Zoe Cross <crushedmarigolds@[omitted].com>
To: Agnes Petrella <agnes_in_wonderland_76@[omitted].com>
Subject: Contract Voided

Agnes,

I'm disheartened to hear of your decision to void our current contract; however, I understand your cause for doing so.

I am truly sorry that I pushed you well beyond your limit. That was never my intention.

I think we both wanted different things out of this relationship and we're coming to the realization that it simply isn't a good fit.

I honor your decision and this email is sent as a voidance of our current contract.

I wish you nothing but health and prosperity in all your future endeavors. I am always here if you need anything.

Best regards,
Zoe

PART FOUR

AN EGG BEFORE
IT CRACKS

EMAIL FROM AGNES PETRELLA

Date: 07/28/2000
Time: 10:01 p.m.
From: Agnes Petrella <agnes_in_wonderland_76@[omitted].com>
To: Zoe Cross <crushedmarigolds@[omitted].com>
Subject: An Apology I Owe You

Hey,

I understand if you'd rather not talk to me after the way I left things over a month ago. But I've been thinking so much about you lately.

It probably doesn't help that I have the apple peeler pinned to my kitchen wall. There were so many times I had contemplated whether or not I should just send it to you with a note telling you how sorry I am.

But I worried you might toss out the box before you even opened it.

Not that you don't have a right to be mad. You are well within reason to not want to talk to me, or to simply tell me to fuck off. Of course, I hope you don't do those things. But what I'm trying to say is that I understand if that's how you feel. I did something to you I'll never forgive myself for as long as I live. After all your consideration, your kindness—to have it thrown back in your face with the same disregard that people might consider when contemplating weekly trash disposal. There's no worse insult I can think of.

It was never my intention to hurt you. I don't really think I'm better off without you. I should've never said that. Sometimes we say or do things to people we love because we know it will hurt them.

Besides, what I had done nearly isn't as horrible as what some other people have done.

For God's sake, there are people who impale baby birds with toothpicks. Or people who pour bleach inside cats' ears.

I don't know about you but hearing about the terrible things other people have done have always made me feel better about the things I've done.

I remember watching a TV interview with a teenager who had crucified his little brother. You probably heard about it. He called his brother "The Little Christ" because his parents endlessly doted on the child.

Anyway, they had him in handcuffs on TV—dressed in an orange jumpsuit, chatting with a reporter. And he starts talking about how he did it.

He waits until his parents go to sleep one night, and he creeps into the nursery, spooning his baby brother from his cradle into his arms. The child makes little mewling noises like a kitten, but he keeps a blanket over his mouth to muffle the sounds. After he's finished loading up the car with the supplies he needs, he ferries the Little Christ from the house to the back seat of his station-wagon. He shifts the car into gear and before long he's on the road, hurtling down the highway as if he were bound for the Promised Land, Shangri-La—anywhere but here.

He thinks about how he should do it first. Should he just kill him and get it over with? Or should he take his time and make it as perfect as possible?

So, after driving for about half an hour, they arrive at the rock quarry on the outskirts of town. He drives to the small ledge overlooking the nearby park where those evangelists built a giant crucifix out of unused pine. So, he pulls the Little Christ out of the car seat and hauls him up toward the cross. The crucifix isn't very large. Maybe six feet tall at most. So, he positions the Little Christ against it—splaying his limbs out against the wood. The child struggles a little. He looks around confused, bands of drool collecting in the corners of his little mouth.

It's now or never, he thinks to himself.

So, he reaches inside the rucksack he's brought with him and he pulls out a hammer and a small nail. He presses the Little Christ's hand against the arm of the cross and that's when he starts to cry, as if the child somehow realizes what he's about to do. Whether he knows his fate before it happens or not, it soon becomes clear to him when he swings the hammer down and smashes the nail through the palm of his little hand. He shrieks as if he were a wounded animal. It sounds almost—inhuman. Pitiful. Like the final pathetic cry of a dying species—a breed on the verge of being swallowed by oblivion.

He can't stop now.

He's already gone too far.

Blood's leaking from the hole he's opened in the Little

Christ's hand. So, he holds him up to keep him from falling and he rummages through his rucksack again until he finds another nail. He stretches his other hand along the other arm of the cross and smashes the hammer down until the nail disappears in a bubble of blood. He removes his hands from him, and he lets the child dangle there, his palms tearing gently under the weight of being held up by the small nails. The Little Christ hangs there, screaming until hoarse—like some sacred offering for an ancient deity. The noise is almost unbearable.

But he's not finished yet.

So, he pulls out a small hunter's knife his father had given him for his twelfth birthday. He slices the baby's belly open until a thin line of blood creeps from the tiny hole he had opened there. It's finished. He doesn't have a crown of thorns to complete the likeness, but he thinks the Little Christ doesn't deserve one.

Once he's finished arranging the child on the cross, braiding ropes around his arms to keep him from falling, he returns to the car to retrieve his paint supplies. He sets his easel up in a small area not far from the cross and as the dawn breaks, he begins to work on his painting. It's not long before the Little Christ's screams dim until they're soundless, his head lowering as if in prayer. He doesn't bother to check. But he knows he's dead.

He doesn't remember what happens next until he sees flashing lights—red and blue—idling toward his car on the quarry's ledge.

The interviewer asks the teenager, "If you could see your baby brother again, what would you say to him?"

The teenager inhales, as if thinking deeply. Then, quite matter-of-factly, he stares straight ahead at the interviewer with a blank expression and says one word: "Nothing."

I could never dream of being a monster like that.

Neither of us are monsters.

Don't we deserve a second chance?

I hope you'll accept this email as my apology and—if you're willing, of course—I hope you'll accept me as your Drudge once more to be faithful to you and to give myself entirely to you.

I'll be waiting for your email.

Love,
Agnes

EMAIL FROM AGNES PETRELLA

Date: 07/30/2000
Time: 11:37 p.m.
From: Agnes Petrella <agnes_in_wonderland_76@[omitted].com>
To: Zoe Cross <crushedmarigolds@[omitted].com>
Subject: Re: An Apology I Owe You

Please write back. I promise to dedicate myself entirely to you.

I'm not better off without you.

I wrote you that story about "The Little Christ" because I wanted to show you there are worse people in the world. We don't belong in their company. We belong together. I know we do.

Agnes

EMAIL FROM ZOE CROSS

Date: 07/31/2000
Time: 8:32 p.m.
From: Zoe Cross <crushedmarigolds@[omitted].com>
To: Agnes Petrella <agnes_in_wonderland_76@[omitted].com>
Subject: Re: An Apology I Owe You

Agnes,

I'm sorry if I've been keeping you on edge the past few days since you sent your first email. I've been unexpectedly busy at work, and I've been trying my best to stay afloat while juggling so many different projects.

I, of course, accept your apology. I was hoping you would eventually reach out as I've been thinking of you a lot lately as well.

I agree to resuming our contract and moving forward with your proposal. I don't necessarily think we need to agree to the contract again as we both understand the consequences of going against what the document stipulates.

However, I do want it known that I require full obedience and honesty if this relationship is to thrive. Any disloyalty, deceit, or noncompliance will be met with a termination of the contract, and we will once again go our separate ways.

I'll be on Instant Messenger tomorrow night at eleven. We can discuss more then.

Yours,
Zoe

INSTANT MESSAGING CONVERSATION
BETWEEN AGNES AND ZOE

07/31/2000
[<crushedmarigolds> has entered the chat]
[<agnes_in_wonderland_76> has entered the chat]

11:00:32 <crushedmarigolds> Hey

11:00:49 <crushedmarigolds> Right on time

11:00:57 <agnes_in_wonderland_76> I told you things would be different now

11:01:05 <crushedmarigolds> Yes. I'm glad

11:01:12 <crushedmarigolds> Glad you're here

11:01:19 <crushedmarigolds> Glad you came back

11:01:25 <agnes_in_wonderland_76> I could never stay away from you

11:01:37 <agnes_in_wonderland_76> You're the only person in my life who hasn't asked me to leave

11:01:46 <crushedmarigolds> Why would I do that?

11:01:58 <agnes_in_wonderland_76> When I was little, I thought if people hurt you, it meant that they loved you

11:02:04 <crushedmarigolds> What made you think that?

11:02:19 <agnes_in_wonderland_76> My parents worked a lot

when I was younger, and they asked my aunt to look after me while they were out

11:02:38 <agnes_in_wonderland_76> My aunt used to play a game with me to keep me quiet, keep me out of the way. She would make me hold an egg and send me into a locked broom closet

11:02:54 <agnes_in_wonderland_76> She used to make me stand in there, holding the egg for hours on end. When it was time to come out, she used to inspect the egg and make sure it hadn't cracked

11:02:13 <agnes_in_wonderland_76> If it had cracked, she used to make me eat it. Every last drop. Even the shell

11:02:29 <agnes_in_wonderland_76> I'd stand there crying, egg smeared all over my face. And she'd say, "I only do this because there are people out there who will do far worse to you"

11:02:38 <agnes_in_wonderland_76> I guess that's what makes people do horrible things—they think whatever they're doing isn't nearly as bad as what somebody else will do

11:02:50 <crushedmarigolds> I would never do anything horrible to you

11:03:01 <agnes_in_wonderland_76> I know you wouldn't

11:03:12 <crushedmarigolds> Everything I've asked of you, I've made you do—it's been from a place of love

11:03:19 <agnes_in_wonderland_76> I know it has

11:03:28 <agnes_in_wonderland_76> That's why I came back

11:03:39 <agnes_in_wonderland_76> Someone else would do far worse things to me

11:03:48 <crushedmarigolds> I would never let that happen

11:03:56 <crushedmarigolds> We made an arrangement.
Remember?

11:04:03 <agnes_in_wonderland_76> Yes

11:04:11 <agnes_in_wonderland_76> Do you ever worry you'll
hurt me?

11:04:16 <crushedmarigolds> Sometimes

11:04:22 <crushedmarigolds> I once dreamt about killing
you

11:04:39 <crushedmarigolds> It wasn't one of those dreams
you wake up from in a cold sweat, heart pumping like
an engine—feeling like you've just run headfirst into
a concrete wall. Skull cracked open and juices leaking
everywhere

11:05:03 <crushedmarigolds> And it definitely wasn't one of
those dreams where you wake up and find the place
between your legs wetting, thighs clenching at the mere
reminder of the memory. Wasn't even a dream you
remember when you first wake up. It was something
that came to me over time, slowly crawling around
inside my head like a beetle—circling some invisible
drain fixed inside there and making its way down into
the sludge where memories collect

11:05:32 <crushedmarigolds> In the dream, you didn't speak

11:05:37 <crushedmarigolds> You couldn't

11:05:59 <crushedmarigolds> In the way that all dreams
give you supernatural powers—abilities beyond
comprehension or even logic—I was able to make you
mute. Mouth could open, but no sound could come out.
When I asked you why you couldn't speak, you gestured
to my hand. It was then that I realized I had ripped out

your tongue and it wiggled between my fingers like a rubbery slice of uncooked meat

11:06:09 <crushedmarigolds> You had showed up on my front porch, suitcase in hand

11:06:34 <crushedmarigolds> I asked you what you're doing here. You tell me you have nowhere else to go

11:07:04 <crushedmarigolds> Before I can challenge you again, there's a horrible explosion outside. I go to the window to look and I'm greeted by a desolate wasteland. The front lawn—once a beautiful emerald carpet—now merely rusted brown and the edges burning. In the distance, a giant mushroom cloud rises into sight. The light around us dims as if the hand of God had drawn a dark curtain over the world. The windows to the house explode, a glittering hailstorm of glass flutters around us like a snow squall

11:07:35 <crushedmarigolds> I suddenly realize you're gone, and it's then I'm approached by a nurse and she tells me that you're upstairs waiting for me

11:07:45 <crushedmarigolds> "Upstairs?" I say

11:08:09 <crushedmarigolds> So, I walk up the stairs to the master bedroom and somehow, I already have the key to unlock the door. I open it and it's not the master bedroom, but a giant hospital room instead. It looks like a place where they do experiments—crimes against nature—like arranging the head of a hamster on the body of a Burmese python. Something atrocious like that

11:08:44 <crushedmarigolds> So, I inch further into the room, and I see you in the hospital bed. Only difference is all your skin has been burned off. Your arms and legs—they look like thin tubes of blood sausage with the transparent casing still on them. Your face—half-melted and dripping like the wax from a candle. Your skin—shining from the radiation and so transparent that I can practically see myself in the reflection. You look so strange and yet—so mesmerizing

11:08:58 <crushedmarigolds> Tubes and wires are connected to your fingers, snaking in and out of your mouth and nostrils. A desperate effort to keep you alive any way possible. Keep you permanently living in your agony

11:10:08 <crushedmarigolds> I inch closer toward the bed to look at you and for some reason, I savor the moment—I savor the sight of you in pain, your eyes pleading with me to end your suffering. I think to myself, "If I were an ice pick, I'd scramble your brain like a plate of eggs." I think to myself, "If I were a black hole, I'd swallow you and shit you out in tiny pieces." I think to myself, "If I were a tomahawk, I'd split you right down the middle like a rotten piece of fruit." I'd do anything I could to erase you—smear you against the world the way a boot wipes off a squished worm on a scraper

11:10:31 <crushedmarigolds> You motion for me to lean closer. So, I do. You can't speak, but I see your lips moving with muted words

11:10:49 <crushedmarigolds> And you mouth the words to me—"Kill me," you say. Over and over again. "Kill me." "KILL ME"

11:10:59 <crushedmarigolds> "With what?" I ask

11:11:52 <crushedmarigolds> Your eyes merely wander to the

machine keeping you alive beside your bed. I follow your eyes and it's then I see the plug in the wall. I don't hesitate at all. One yank and it's decided. The line flattens on the screen. Doctors and nurses, their faces hidden behind surgical masks, rush into the room and examine you. They don't do much. Merely shut your eyelids before passing a white sheet over your face. Then, they turn to me

11:12:09 <crushedmarigolds> "You have to take her place now," they say to me

11:12:20 <crushedmarigolds> "But, I'm not sick," I say. "Look at me. I'm fine"

11:12:43 <crushedmarigolds> Then, I look down and I realize my skin has been burned off too—shining tissue blistered red staring back at me in my skin's reflection. It's not long before I take your place—reclining in the bed, machines keeping me alive

11:13:03 <crushedmarigolds> Only this time, there's nobody around to pull the plug for me

11:13:45 <crushedmarigolds> Are you still there?

11:13:58 <agnes_in_wonderland_76> Yeah, I'm here

11:14:09 <crushedmarigolds> Dreams can tell us things

11:14:13 <agnes_in_wonderland_76> What did that dream tell you?

11:14:23 <crushedmarigolds> How I would never want to hurt you

11:14:44 <agnes_in_wonderland_76> Yes

11:14:49 <crushedmarigolds> Also how much I love you

11:14:59 <agnes_in_wonderland_76> Love?

11:15:07 <crushedmarigolds> Does that word scare you?

11:15:09 <agnes_in_wonderland_76> No, I like it. It sounds nice

11:15:17 <crushedmarigolds> I can't stay on. Early workday tomorrow

11:15:28 <agnes_in_wonderland_76> You'll email me?

11:15:38 <crushedmarigolds> Why wouldn't I?

11:15:44 <agnes_in_wonderland_76> Good

11:15:49 <agnes_in_wonderland_76> I love you

11:15:55 <crushedmarigolds> Love you

[<crushedmarigolds> has left the chat]

[<agnes_in_wonderland_76> has left the chat]

EMAIL FROM AGNES PETRELLA

Date: 08/01/2000

Time: 10:09 a.m.

From: Agnes Petrella <agnes_in_wonderland_76@[omitted].com>

To: Zoe Cross <crushedmarigolds@[omitted].com>

Subject: I've been thinking…

I've been thinking a lot about our conversation the other night, and I don't want to leave any opportunity for vagueness.

I promised myself I would live unapologetically and damn anybody who finds it offensive.

I need to be as candid with you as I can possibly be. I, at the very least, owe you my honesty.

I want us to have a baby.

I know what you're thinking. I know you probably think I'm crazy, but I've been thinking about this for quite some time, and I think it's only natural for the two of us to create life together.

We love one another, don't we?

We belong together.

I want to carry your life in me.

I, of course, haven't considered the details. But all I know is I want to make this happen between us. I *need* to make this happen.

What do you think?

EMAIL FROM ZOE CROSS

Date: 08/01/2000
Time: 5:12 p.m.
From: Zoe Cross <crushedmarigolds@[omitted].com>
To: Agnes Petrella <agnes_in_wonderland_76@[omitted].com>
Subject: Re: I've been thinking...

Agnes,

I've been thinking about your email all day.

I don't quite know how to respond, and I certainly hope I don't come across as uncaring given the brevity of this email I'm writing.

Of course, I love you. Of course, I would want to have a child with you.

But it's just not possible right now. I don't know if it ever will be, but I know for certain that it's something I can't accept ownership of at the moment.

I so desperately wish I could give you exactly what you desire.

I've been thinking, too—thinking of ways we both can get what we want.

I think I've come up with a solution, but I'm apprehensive

to share my idea over email. I was hoping we could chat on Instant Messenger again tonight so I can share my idea with you.

Don't worry, my love. The agony of uncertainty won't last for long.

Zoe

INSTANT MESSAGING CONVERSATION
BETWEEN AGNES AND ZOE

08/01/2000

[<crushedmarigolds> has entered the chat]

[<agnes_in_wonderland_76> has entered the chat]

10:32:02 <crushedmarigolds> Hey

10:32:09 <agnes_in_wonderland_76> Hey

10:32:18 <crushedmarigolds> You're not upset, are you?

10:32:29 <agnes_in_wonderland_76> I'm bracing myself for the worst

10:32:34 <crushedmarigolds> And why's that?

10:32:41 <agnes_in_wonderland_76> You don't want to have a baby with me

10:32:54 <crushedmarigolds> That's not true

10:33:04 <crushedmarigolds> You know that's not true

10:33:12 <crushedmarigolds> I'd give anything to be able to give you exactly what you want

10:33:23 <crushedmarigolds> It's just not possible right now

10:33:35 <agnes_in_wonderland_76> I know

10:33:42 <crushedmarigolds> But, there's something you can do

10:33:53 <crushedmarigolds> If you're serious about wanting to carry life inside you

10:33:59 <agnes_in_wonderland_76> Yes

10:34:13 <crushedmarigolds> You're certain you're serious?

10:34:24 <agnes_in_wonderland_76> I want it more than anything

10:34:26 <crushedmarigolds> Then, you have to get sick

10:34:29 <agnes_in_wonderland_76> Get sick?

10:34:33 <crushedmarigolds> Yes

10:34:44 <agnes_in_wonderland_76> Sick with what?

10:34:56 <crushedmarigolds> What exactly is a baby? Before it's born?

10:35:04 <agnes_in_wonderland_76> What do you mean?

10:35:08 <crushedmarigolds> It lives off a host body, like a parasite

10:35:13 <agnes_in_wonderland_76> I suppose

10:35:28 <crushedmarigolds> A child is an infection

10:35:34 <crushedmarigolds> Like a parasite

10:35:45 <agnes_in_wonderland_76> You're saying…?

10:35:55 <crushedmarigolds> You must become infected

10:36:04 <crushedmarigolds> Become infected with a parasite and carry the creature as if it were your child

10:36:08 <agnes_in_wonderland_76> Will it hurt?

10:36:16 <crushedmarigolds> Change always hurts

10:36:24 <crushedmarigolds> But it will give you the life you've always wanted to carry inside you

10:36:35 <agnes_in_wonderland_76> You're certain it's the only way?

10:36:42 <crushedmarigolds> It would give you exactly what you wanted

10:36:55 <agnes_in_wonderland_76> How do you know?

10:37:12 <crushedmarigolds> I contracted a tapeworm in college during a trip to Cambodia. I know what it feels like

10:37:23 <agnes_in_wonderland_76> What did it feel like?

10:37:35 <crushedmarigolds> Feels like you're living for something else. Makes you feel like a god, carrying something alive inside you

10:37:44 <agnes_in_wonderland_76> Yes, that's what I wanted it to feel like

10:37:52 <crushedmarigolds> You'll think about it?

10:38:03 <agnes_in_wonderland_76> Yes

10:38:09 <agnes_in_wonderland_76> I'll think about it

10:38:16 <crushedmarigolds> I'll love you no matter what

10:38:25 <agnes_in_wonderland_76> I'll love you, too

10:38:37 <agnes_in_wonderland_76> No matter what

[<crushedmarigolds> has left the chat]
[<agnes_in_wonderland_76> has left the chat]

EMAIL FROM AGNES PETRELLA

Date: 08/02/2000
Time: 7:41 a.m.
From: Agnes Petrella <agnes_in_wonderland_76@[omitted].com>
To: Zoe Cross <crushedmarigolds@[omitted].com>
Subject: Re: Our Conversation Last Night

Zoe,

I'll do it.

    Love,
    Agnes

ZOE CROSS

Date: 08/02/2000
Time: 10:08 a.m.
From: Zoe Cross <crushedmarigolds@[omitted].com>
To: Agnes Petrella <agnes_in_wonderland_76@[omitted].com>
Subject: Re: Our Conversation Last Night

Good. I'm glad to hear it.

Now, we have to be as precise as possible when executing this plan.

It's not as simple as going to your local butcher and asking for his leanest cut of beef tenderloin. There's, of course, the possibility this won't work and will negatively impact your health.

If you're serious about going forward with this, then you're going to have to neglect any semblance of hygiene or formality when preparing to eat.

Of course, there are methods by which doctors can remove parasites from their human host; however, there's no conclusive way to actually contract the organism.

So, much of what I'm about to tell you is in no way a conclusive way to contract a parasite, but rather ways by which a host may become infected with a parasite.

You'll need to go to your local town market and ask for a pound of uncooked pork. After you've acquired the meat, you need to return home and leave the pork in a place where it won't be disturbed. Leave it outside.

It won't be long before all kinds of insects will arrive, a glittering haze swallowing the portion of meat until they've finally nourished themselves and laid their eggs deep in its brawn.

After two days of waiting, you're to go outside and locate the sun-cooked meat.

Though it may disgust you, you're to take a knife and fork and hack through the uncooked pork, slice off a small piece, and consume it.

You're to do this until the meat is completely gone and you're fully fed.

You may want to throw up after you've eaten. You may feel as though you need to. I urge you to keep as much of it down as possible—that's the only way this will work.

And, of course, you want this to work, don't you?

EMAIL FROM AGNES PETRELLA

Date: 08/05/2000

Time: 9:07 p.m.

From: Agnes Petrella <agnes_in_wonderland_76@[omitted].com>

To: Zoe Cross <crushedmarigolds@[omitted].com>

Subject: It's finished

It's over now. The worst part is behind me.

Chewing on that—the way the little eggs burst between my teeth like sunflower seeds. I'm getting ahead of myself. I'll bet you want to know how it happened.

I did exactly what you said. I went into town and visited the local market—a horrible place I worked over the summer when I was a teenager. Haven't been there in several years, but I remember the butcher there—this giant man with a pockmarked face dressed in a bloodstained apron.

He greeted me at the counter.

"How's your mother?" he asked, leaning over and exposing the dark stains beneath both of his arms.

I made some bland comment about how well she's been (after all, how am I supposed to know?), and I asked him how his daughters are—I remember they were in preschool when I worked there.

When we were finally past the painful pleasantries, I asked him for a cut of pork.

"Just the one?" he asked me.

I nodded.

When he was done packaging it, it was as neatly packaged as a Christmas present. I recall marveling at the wrapping paper. I remember how when I was little, I thought exquisitely wrapped slices of meat resembled something too graceful to eat, as if it were the organ of an angel—the innards of some divine being far too consecrated to consume.

I returned home and I unwrapped the meat from its packaging. It was as dark red as some rare tropical plant. I lifted the piece of meat from the counter, inhaling its scent. I imagined myself biting into it, my teeth chewing through the toughness as matter separated as if it were damp cotton.

I threw the pork on a dinner plate and crept outside into the backyard where I set it down behind a small tree near the fence.

Then, I waited.

Every morning I would go to the kitchen window and watch as little bugs swarmed over the fresh plate of meat, a dim cloud of insects collecting as if it were carrion's shadow—tiny winged mourners to prepare and embalm the recently deceased.

Finally, at the end of the second day, I made my way out to the tree and half expected the plate to be gone completely thanks to one of nature's little trespassers. But, miraculously, it was still there.

After swatting away some of the flies glued to the meat,

I ferried it back into the kitchen and started to inspect my meal.

The sun had drained it of most of its color, little thatches of blight creeping along the edges of the uncooked pork. Ribbons of exposed tissue sprouted along the meat's surface like slashes from a knife on human skin and burrowing deep inside the yawning crevices were white maggots.

I nearly retched at the sight.

But I thought of you and knew you would want me to go through with it.

So, I took a knife and fork from the cupboard and sawed through the uncooked pork. When I was finished, I speared the piece with my fork. It was then that I noticed a tiny maggot—no bigger than the tip of a dressmaker's thimble— squirming across the piece of meat.

Even a carcass can carry life, so why not me?

Before I allowed my mind to wander too freely, I took a bite. It was like chewing on cooked rubber, little maggots squishing like jelly between my teeth as I gnawed.

I took another bite. And then, another.

I vomited once.

But I kept eating. Just like you told me to.

Finally, the plate was clear.

I swallowed, my whole body shuddering at the acrid taste.

Now, I suppose we wait. That's all we can do.

Just think, everything could be different for me tomorrow. My whole life could change. I hope it does.

EMAIL FROM ZOE CROSS

Date: 08/07/2000
Time: 8:33 a.m.
From: Zoe Cross <crushedmarigolds@[omitted].com>
To: Agnes Petrella <agnes_in_wonderland_76@[omitted].com>
Subject: Re: It's finished

Hey,

You weren't on Instant Messenger last night. I waited for you.

Is everything OK?

I've been thinking of you.

I still can't quite believe you went through with it. I never thought you would. I thought you'd ask to not see me again or tell me off when I first suggested it.

But you want this bad enough. I can tell.

Write me back so I know you're OK.

Love,
Zoe

EMAIL FROM AGNES PETRELLA

Date: 08/08/2000
Time: 6:41 p.m.
From: Agnes Petrella <agnes_in_wonderland_76@[omitted].com>
To: Zoe Cross <crushedmarigolds@[omitted].com>
Subject: Re: It's finished

It didn't work.

After everything I've done, and it didn't work.

My roommate took me to the hospital the other night because I couldn't stop vomiting. They ran a bunch of tests and kept me there for observation. But I don't think it's happened.

They would've told me, right?

They would've seen some sign—something in the tests. I don't know how quickly it works or what it might show up as, but they would've told me if they found something inside me after so many tests.

There's no point to anything.

It doesn't matter. It's always never mattered.

Did I ever tell you the one about the cat and the priest?

You know, it's been so cold lately. I read somewhere online that you should always check underneath your car before you start it because sometimes little animals like to nest under there to get warm.

Well, my roommate was working late one night, and we needed bread and eggs. So, I got in the car and drove down the street to the market on the corner of Ashworth and Beaumont. Picked up the bread and eggs—and a few other things I needed.

As I'm walking through the store, I notice there's a priest, dressed in his robes, also shopping.

He's dressed in expensive-looking black and has the white collar around his neck. He looks so out of place in this labyrinth of linoleum and fluorescent lighting, like a lost member of some celestial court.

So, I start to follow him through the store. I don't know why. I just do.

I'm about to go up to him and say something—I have no idea what I'm going to say—but he dashes to the Express checkout line before I can get his attention. So, after I'm done buying my groceries, I try to catch him out at his car in the parking lot.

But, once again, he's too quick for me and he's already ducking into the driver's seat. I happen to glance beneath his car because I see something moving there in the light.

Something curled beneath one of the tires.

It's a stray cat with a bright orange tail. I wave at him to stop, but he doesn't see me. And the car's tires slide right over the cat.

The cat lies there, dead. Ropes of its intestines pushed out through its open mouth. Its ribcage—flattened like a sheet of paper.

I wave at the priest. "Stop. Please."

He does. Rolls down the window. I say, "You just ran over this poor cat."

He doesn't even bother to look at it. He merely looks at me and asks, "Does it matter?"

And with that, he cranks up his window and speeds off down the lane. And as I'm left standing there with the squeezed out remains of that dead cat, I wonder to myself, "Does it matter? Does any of this really matter?"

The answer's no.

The answer's always been no.

PART FIVE

GRACIOUS HOST

EMAIL FROM AGNES PETRELLA

Date: 08/12/2000
Time: 11:29 a.m.
From: Agnes Petrella <agnes_in_wonderland_76@[omitted].com>
To: Zoe Cross <crushedmarigolds@[omitted].com>
Subject: Things may be changing

It may be finally happening for us.

I woke up this morning and found myself unable to pull myself away from kneeling before the toilet.

I have the most intense abdominal pain I've ever felt. Worse than my usual period cramps. It feels like a cat's claw raking through my insides and readjusting what it finds there.

I think it's finally happened: I'm carrying life inside me.

It's yours, too.

Ours.

EMAIL FROM ZOE CROSS

Date: 08/12/2000

Time: 1:17 p.m.

From: Zoe Cross <crushedmarigolds@[omitted].com>

To: Agnes Petrella <agnes_in_wonderland_76@[omitted].com>

Subject: Re: Things may be changing

Agnes,

I'm delighted to hear you're so optimistic about everything. It sounds promising, from what I can tell.

You very well could be hosting a parasite now.

The only way to actually be certain of the infection is to consult with your primary care physician.

I would make an appointment with him or her as soon as possible.

Zoe

EMAIL FROM AGNES PETRELLA

Date: 08/12/2000
Time: 2:32 p.m.
From: Agnes Petrella <agnes_in_wonderland_76@[omitted].com>
To: Zoe Cross <crushedmarigolds@[omitted].com>
Subject: Re: Things may be changing

Are you happy, my love? Please tell me you are.

EMAIL FROM ZOE CROSS

Date: 08/12/2000

Time: 3:19 p.m.

From: Zoe Cross <crushedmarigolds@[omitted].com>

To: Agnes Petrella <agnes_in_wonderland_76@[omitted].com>

Subject: Re: Things may be changing

I'm happy if you are, my love. That's all that matters.
Let me know what the doctor says.

EMAIL FROM AGNES PETRELLA

Date: 08/15/2000

Time: 3:54 p.m.

From: Agnes Petrella <agnes_in_wonderland_76@[omitted].com>

To: Zoe Cross <crushedmarigolds@[omitted].com>

Subject: It's a boy

It's real. I can hardly believe it.

I had to sit down and compose myself when the doctor first told me.

There's a living thing inside me.

And it's ours, my love.

It's ours.

They ran some more tests—bloodwork, a stool sample, etc. And that's when the doctor came into the room and explained I'm the host to a tapeworm.

Our child.

I know tapeworms are technically hermaphrodites and have both male and female sex organs, but wouldn't it be nice to think of it as a boy?

A son.

Our little family.

We could name him whatever we please.

What do you think of the name Finneas? I suppose we have time to think and pick out the most perfect name for our child.

I can hardly contain my excitement.

It's what I've wanted my whole life. I hope you're happy, too.

I'm sure you are.

I'll be on Instant Messenger later tonight. We can talk about names and everything else then.

Thank you for everything, my love.

Thank you for making me a mother.

INSTANT MESSAGING CONVERSATION BETWEEN AGNES AND ZOE

08/15/2000

[<crushedmarigolds> has entered the chat]
[<agnes_in_wonderland_76> has entered the chat]

10:09:12 <agnes_in_wonderland_76> You're going to be a mother!

10:09:18 <agnes_in_wonderland_76> Can you believe it?

10:09:30 <crushedmarigolds> Are you happy?

10:09:48 <agnes_in_wonderland_76> How can you even ask that? You already know I'm ecstatic. Over the moon

10:09:56 <agnes_in_wonderland_76> Do you know what I did today?

10:10:03 <crushedmarigolds> What?

10:10:12 <agnes_in_wonderland_76> I sang

10:10:14 <agnes_in_wonderland_76> In public

10:10:19 <agnes_in_wonderland_76> People were listening, and I didn't care

10:10:26 <agnes_in_wonderland_76> I feel wonderful. The best I've felt in years. All because of you

10:10:34 <crushedmarigolds> What did the doctor say?

10:10:39 <agnes_in_wonderland_76> He prescribed me some meds

10:10:45 <agnes_in_wonderland_76> I'm not going to take them, of course

10:10:49 <agnes_in_wonderland_76> They want to kill our child

10:10:59 <agnes_in_wonderland_76> I don't even want to go out anymore

10:11:05 <crushedmarigolds> Why's that?

10:11:09 <agnes_in_wonderland_76> I want to be with you and our baby

10:11:16 <agnes_in_wonderland_76> The three of us together

10:11:22 <crushedmarigolds> But what about…

10:11:29 <agnes_in_wonderland_76> Yes?

10:11:38 <crushedmarigolds> What about when your body finally passes the tapeworm?

10:11:44 <agnes_in_wonderland_76> That's not going to happen

10:11:49 <crushedmarigolds> It's not?

10:12:02 <agnes_in_wonderland_76> I'm going to carry our child forever. He's going to always be a part of me

10:12:09 <agnes_in_wonderland_76> That's how it's going to be, isn't it?

10:12:14 <agnes_in_wonderland_76> I'll always have a part of you inside me

10:12:19 <crushedmarigolds> But that's not the way it works

10:12:24 <agnes_in_wonderland_76> What are you trying to say?

10:12:35 <crushedmarigolds> Eventually it'll pass

10:12:46 <crushedmarigolds> You can't play the "gracious host" forever

10:12:57 <agnes_in_wonderland_76> Are you not happy?

10:13:05 <agnes_in_wonderland_76> I thought you would be

10:13:09 <crushedmarigolds> Of course, I'm happy

10:13:17 <crushedmarigolds> This is what you wanted, after all

10:13:22 <crushedmarigolds> But I don't want you to be hurt

10:13:29 <agnes_in_wonderland_76> I know you'd never hurt me

10:13:37 <crushedmarigolds> When it leaves you

10:13:44 <agnes_in_wonderland_76> It's not going to leave me

10:13:49 <agnes_in_wonderland_76> I'm going to keep it forever

10:14:09 <agnes_in_wonderland_76> Sometimes I imagine the three of us lying in bed together—your arms wrapped around me, our beloved little worm curled like a cold, wet rope on my stomach

10:14:19 <agnes_in_wonderland_76> Wouldn't that be perfect?

10:14:27 <agnes_in_wonderland_76> Don't you dream of those things too?

10:14:35 <crushedmarigolds> I haven't been dreaming lately

10:14:45 <crushedmarigolds> I have to go get some sleep

10:14:27 <agnes_in_wonderland_76> Can't you stay?

10:14:32 <agnes_in_wonderland_76> Five more minutes?

10:14:43 <crushedmarigolds> We'll talk tomorrow. I'll send you an email

10:14:48 <agnes_in_wonderland_76> You still love me?

10:14:55 <crushedmarigolds> Yes

10:14:59 <agnes_in_wonderland_76> I love you, too

10:15:02 <agnes_in_wonderland_76> The both of us do

[<crushedmarigolds> has left the chat]

[<agnes_in_wonderland_76> has left the chat]

EMAIL FROM ZOE CROSS

Date: 08/16/2000

Time: 12:17 p.m.

From: Zoe Cross <crushedmarigolds@[omitted].com>

To: Agnes Petrella <agnes_in_wonderland_76@[omitted].com>

Subject: I'm having second thoughts

Agnes,

This isn't an easy email for me to write. I'm afraid none of this gives me any semblance of pleasure.

If I expect total honesty and obedience from you, then you, at the very least, deserve the same amount of trustworthiness from me.

The truth is, I'm worried about you. Not only your physical health, but your mental well-being as well.

If I'm being totally honest with you—some of the things I've made you do have been rooted in a place of selfishness. Some of the things I've made you do have been a result of my whims—placing bets on your endurance and wondering how far you'll go before you break.

You've proved me wrong several times, and I'm afraid much of the hardship was at your expense.

I'm not a good person. Not as good a person as you are.

I'm ashamed to admit it, but you deserve someone who won't pretend to care for you while they are meanwhile banking on your misfortune.

Because of this, I'm thinking of ending things between us for the foreseeable future.

I know you're going to be upset. But this is for the best. I ask you to trust me.

I know I certainly don't deserve any trust given my capriciousness, but I know in time you'll come to recognize that I'm trying to help you. For the first time I'm thinking of someone other than myself. It scares me.

But letting something happen to you scares me even more.

The sad truth is I don't think I love you as much as you love me. And that's OK. That happens in relationships all the time—there's always someone who loves more than the other.

But I can't take ownership of your destruction. I want this to stop.

EMAIL FROM AGNES PETRELLA

Date: 08/16/2000

Time: 2:08 p.m.

From: Agnes Petrella <agnes_in_wonderland_76@[omitted].com>

To: Zoe Cross <crushedmarigolds@[omitted].com>

Subject: Re: I'm having second thoughts

Fuck your second thoughts.

Fuck your honesty. I don't need your honesty. I need your love, and I foolishly thought it was mine all this time.

I can't believe you're doing this to me.

I'm not some car battery you use for a couple thousand miles and then send off to the junkyard, you fucking cunt.

I know exactly what you're trying to do.

You're trying to abandon me with our child. The one you wanted as well.

This life inside me is ours. No matter what you say. No matter what you think.

It's always going to be ours.

EMAIL FROM ZOE CROSS

Date: 08/17/2000

Time: 8:43 a.m.

From: Zoe Cross <crushedmarigolds@[omitted].com>

To: Agnes Petrella <agnes_in_wonderland_76@[omitted].com>

Subject: Re: I'm having second thoughts

I've tried to reason with you and look where it's gotten me.

Agnes, you're sick and you need help.

If you're going to continue to be so monstrous, then I have no choice but to cut all communication with you.

As far as I'm concerned, our contract is null and void.

Do not reach out to me as I will not be responding.

I sincerely hope you get the help that you need.

EMAIL FROM ZOE CROSS

Date: 08/17/2000
Time: 8:56 a.m.
From: Zoe Cross <crushedmarigolds@[omitted].com>
To: Agnes Petrella <agnes_in_wonderland_76@[omitted].com>
Subject: Re: I'm having second thoughts

I think I did once love you.
    I think I could have loved you.
    But not like this.
    Never like this.

EMAIL FROM AGNES PETRELLA

Date: 08/18/2000
Time: 11:09 a.m.
From: Agnes Petrella <agnes_in_wonderland_76@[omitted].com>
To: Zoe Cross <crushedmarigolds@[omitted].com>
Subject: Re: I'm having second thoughts

You'll never leave me. You love me too much.

You love our child too much.

I know you'll respond. You always will.

Because you know the life I'm carrying inside me belongs to you.

I thought of you last night.

I slept without clothes on, as we had agreed upon. The AC was running on full blast.

I didn't even care how cold it was.

I just thought of how it would feel to have you lying next to me—our child coiled inside my stomach.

EMAIL FROM AGNES PETRELLA

Date: 08/19/2000

Time: 7:43 p.m.

From: Agnes Petrella <agnes_in_wonderland_76@[omitted].com>

To: Zoe Cross <crushedmarigolds@[omitted].com>

Subject: Re: I'm having second thoughts

Please respond. It's been days since we last talked.

    I want things to go back to how they were.

    If you'd like me to get help, I'll get it.

    Anything you say.

    Just please talk to me. I can't bear being apart from you.

FROM AGNES PETRELLA

Date: 08/20/2000
Time: 9:33 p.m.
From: Agnes Petrella <agnes_in_wonderland_76@[omitted].com>
To: Zoe Cross <crushedmarigolds@[omitted].com>
Subject: Something's wrong

Things have gotten worse since we last spoke.

I think there's something wrong.

It hurts me to even think it, but something's not right with our child.

I feel this intense pain all the time, as if someone were sliding a razor blade along my guts.

I don't know if I can bear it anymore. I feel like taking a pair of shears and slicing myself open.

Would you come then?

Would that get your attention?

FROM AGNES PETRELLA

Date: 08/21/2000
Time: 6:45 p.m.
From: Agnes Petrella <agnes_in_wonderland_76@[omitted].com>
To: Zoe Cross <crushedmarigolds@[omitted].com>
Subject: Re: Something's wrong

Please help me.

I think something's happening to our child.

It feels like a gloved hand pushing its way through my innards and reaching down between where my legs meet.

Something's going to happen.

EMAIL FROM AGNES PETRELLA

Date: 08/21/2000
Time: 8:02 p.m.
From: Agnes Petrella <agnes_in_wonderland_76@[omitted].com>
To: Zoe Cross <crushedmarigolds@[omitted].com>
Subject: Re: Something's wrong

I passed it. Just like you said.

It's a damp, crumpled heap on the bathroom floor.

Looks like one of the ribbons my mother used to sew into my hair when I was a little girl—shiny and bright.

EMAIL FROM AGNES PETRELLA

Date: 08/21/2000
Time: 8:38 p.m.
From: Agnes Petrella <agnes_in_wonderland_76@[omitted].com>
To: Zoe Cross <crushedmarigolds@[omitted].com>
Subject: Re: Something's wrong

I wish you were here.

He's beautiful.

He has your eyes. And your smile.

I hold him in my arms and pretend he makes little cooing noises at me the way all babies do.

EMAIL FROM AGNES PETRELLA

Date: 08/21/2000
Time: 9:06 p.m.
From: Agnes Petrella <agnes_in_wonderland_76@[omitted].com>
To: Zoe Cross <crushedmarigolds@[omitted].com>
Subject: Re: Something's wrong

I take the apple peeler from the kitchen, and I crawl into the bathroom closet, gently cradling our child.

I pretend I can hear the sound of him faintly breathing.

The peeler trembles in my hand.

I close my eyes, and for a moment I wonder if I truly deserve them today.

THE ENCHANTMENT

For my mother who will always believe

ONE

Olive watches as car headlights shimmer through the foyer window, the white light bleeding across the marble floor.

"Shh. He's coming," she says.

"Are you ready—?" her husband, James, replies as he ducks behind the entryway's walnut credenza.

Olive's ears pin at the noise of car keys jingling, footsteps approaching.

The door unlocks, swinging open to reveal the pockmarked face of a teenage boy. He shivers, a gust of snow clinging to him as he removes his knitted hat. His hands frisk the wall for the light switch.

As soon as his fingers find it: lights on.

Olive and James leap out from hiding, shouting in unison, "Surprise!"

Milo lurches back, clutching his backpack.

"Happy Birthday, Milo," they cheer.

Olive watches her son's face thaw with a half-hearted smile as he realizes, slowly letting his guard down. She sees his eyes glance up at the giant banner pinned above the entryway—"Happy 17th Birthday, Milo," written in exquisite cursive lettering.

With open arms, Olive approaches her teenage son and swaddles him as if he were a child.

"Happy birthday, dear," she says. "We love you."

She senses her son reluctantly lean into the hug, his arms remaining at his side. It wasn't much, but she couldn't ask for anything more.

Or perhaps she could.

Quickly thinking, she snatches a green party hat from the nearby table and straps it to Milo's head.

As always, James interferes, ushering Olive aside and passing Milo a small box wrapped in a bright red bow.

"Happy birthday," he says. "You didn't think we'd forget about you, did you—?"

Milo stammers, unsure. "I don't—I didn't think I'd see you here."

Milo's unsureness pains Olive. How could he possibly think his own parents would forget him? Before she can intercede, James pats Milo on the shoulder in the way that all fathers seem to patronize their sons.

"Wouldn't miss it for the world," he says.

Without another moment of hesitation, Olive swipes the gift from Milo.

"Why don't we leave the presents for later, dear?" she suggests. "We can have cake first."

She pulls the mittens from his hands, guiding him further into the house as if he were a mere visitor.

"He's probably full, Olive," James says. "Let the boy open his gift."

As she pulls Milo by the hand, she does a quick double take. There's something wrong.

"What's this—?" she asks, pulling his hand closer to her face for proper inspection.

She opens his fist, revealing his palm desecrated with a giant black circle as if drawn with permanent marker.

"You're still doing this?" she asks. "Milo. We talked about this."

Before she can chastise him any further, Milo slips out of his mother's grasp and recoils.

"You said he wasn't doing that anymore," James says.

"I thought he wasn't. I've hidden all the markers from him."

"You don't think he can find a permanent marker at school?"

"They're supposed to be watching him," Olive reminds her husband.

"What seventeen-year-old needs someone to be watching him regularly?"

As they bicker, Milo begins to sneak out of the entryway and away from earshot. Out of the corner of her eye, Olive watches her son. As he ducks into the nearby dining room, he passes a giant oil painting mounted on the wall detailing the crucifixion of Jesus Christ.

She observes him for a moment, bewildered, as his eyes seem to linger on the nails driven into Christ's hands and the blood leaking there.

He gazes at the portrait longingly as if it were the first time that he was seeing it, as if it were truly a sight to behold, as if he would give anything to endure such wondrous suffering.

Olive clears the empty plates and glasses from the dining room table, smearing cake frosting across her apron.

In the living room, the television plays, rinsing the walls and furniture with a silver glow. On the screen, a well-coiffed reporter addresses the camera. Text appears in the corner of the screen: "The After Life now an After Thought."

"Reports are still coming in from cities across the world such as Hong Kong, Moscow, Beirut, and Tokyo," the reporter announces. "All cities confirming a substantial spike in the number of suicides presumably related to the news first revealed last week—the first scientific evidence to refute the existence of an afterlife. We now go live to our Chief Correspondent, Everett Singer, with the latest…"

Olive aims the remote at the television and the screen goes dark.

Returning to the dining room table, she watches as James and Milo sit—their eyes avoiding the other with such exact carefulness.

Olive's gaze darts between father and son, as if commanding them to speak.

No such luck.

She presents the gift box James had given Milo earlier.

"Milo. Dear," she says playfully—a mother desperately and shamelessly vying for her son's affection. "Why don't you open the gift your father brought?"

Milo shrugs, eyes listless and attention very much elsewhere.

Olive pushes the gift into her son's hands. "Here."

Milo peels the wrapping paper apart, exposing a white box. He slides the lid off to reveal a hammer with a gólden handle.

Olive frowns, rolling her eyes.

"I thought you could use it to finish that project for school you've been working on," James says quietly.

Milo admires the hammer, its handle glinting in the light. The corners of his mouth pull downward.

"Thanks," he says.

James leans in closer toward his son, as if he were approaching a small, frightened animal. Cautious. Careful of every word. "Maybe... you'll let me see it sometime."

Milo slides the hammer back into the box, visibly casketing the remainder of James's hope for a possible truce.

"Maybe," the sullen seventeen-year-old says.

James deflates, eyes flashing to Olive for assurance. There's none to be had.

Olive watches her son pause. Then, his eyes snap to his father. Hopeful.

"Can you spend the night?" he asks.

James stammers, unsure what to say.

Milo's eyes flash to his mother, begging her. Olive senses her face softening. Of course, she might have deprived him of the request in the past, given the circumstances surrounding her separation from James. But she could hardly convince herself to dispossess her son of everything he might wish for on his birthday.

"It's OK with me," she says. "If it would make you happy."

She watches as James's eyes scour the table for an answer. Or rather, an excuse.

"I—I don't think—that would be a good idea," he says.

Olive notices Milo soften. She senses herself thaw with disappointment as well. Of course, she hadn't expected James to take her up on such an offer. But she thought he might have at least pretended to consider it for longer than he had merely for Milo's sake.

Just then, Milo jumps out of his seat and his eyes dart to Olive.

"May I be excused?" he asks. "I have to go pray."

"Already?" she asks. "Your father just got here. Besides, we haven't played Pictionary yet. Isn't that your favorite?"

Milo flashes her his wristwatch. "It's already eight-thirty. I'm late."

Olive clears her throat, shoulders dropping. Defeated. She knows full well it's a fight she won't win.

"Fine," she says, folding her arms.

Milo grabs the box and darts from the room without even looking at his father.

James's eyes lower as his son leaves. Whether from disappointment or resentment, Olive cannot be certain.

"Don't stay up too late," she says, calling after him.

After the sound of Milo's footsteps drift further away, Olive resumes clearing the plates from the dinner table. She glances at James—his head lowered like a disgraced schoolboy, his mouth permanently frowning.

"I'm sure he loved your present," she says. "He just—hasn't been himself lately. Not since…"

"I know."

Olive, at a loss for what to say, exhales deeply and straightens as if she were stretching from underneath the invisible concrete pillar that had been placed on her backside.

"I'm thinking of taking him to a counselor."

"Another one?" James asks.

Olive shakes her head, unsure.

"Let me talk to him," James says, rising from his seat and tossing his napkin aside.

Just as he's about to leave, Olive swipes at his hand.

"James," she says. "You can spend the night if you want."

She watches him bite his lip until it turns purple—a nervous habit he never seemed to be able to break.

"I'll think about it," he says, shoving his hands into his pockets and hurrying out of the room.

However, Olive already knows full well it's something he'll never consider no matter how much she begs, no matter how much she pleads with him.

This place is no longer his home.

TWO

From the end of the hallway, Olive observes as James knocks on his son's bedroom door, inching into the attic. She watches him scan the room—the high vaulted ceiling, the skylight dripping with light from the moon. His eyes eventually arrive at the room's ornate centerpiece—a gigantic crucifix leaning against the wall beside Milo's unmade bed. Green plastic tarp covers the area of the floor surrounding the cross. Half-empty paint cans litter the space.

James's eyes find Milo huddled in a corner of the room, head bowed and praying.

"…Give us this day our daily bread. And forgive us our trespasses, as we forgive those who trespass against us. And lead us not into temptation, but deliver us from evil. For thine is the kingdom, and the power, and the glory. For ever and ever. Amen."

When he's finished with the prayer, Milo blesses himself with the sign of the cross—his eyes revering the crucifix staring down at him.

From the slivered doorway, Olive watches her husband approach Milo gently.

"So, this is the school project. Huh?"

Milo grunts, kneeling and dipping a brush into one of the nearby cans of paint. "Not finished with it yet. Still have to paint it."

"How do you plan on getting this thing into school?" James asks.

"One of my buddies has a pickup truck," Milo says. "Said he'd help me if I gave him some gas money."

Olive watches as James uncomfortably folds his arms and circles his son.

"Looks like you don't really need the hammer," James says. "Always next time, I guess."

Milo merely ignores him and continues his labor with the red paint.

James paces back and forth, visibly searching his mind for something.

"You pray like that every day?" he asks.

Milo glares at his father. "Five times a day. Don't you?"

"I'm… surprised you're still so devout… with everything that's going on. Don't your friends say anything to you?"

Milo shrugs, dipping his paintbrush in the can once more. "Yeah. But I don't listen. Just like the news. I don't listen to that either. Mom says I shouldn't."

"Yes. She's right," James says. "It's your choice to think whatever—"

"It's not what I think," Milo says dangerously. "It's what's true."

Then, he resumes work on the life-size crucifix.

James sits on the edge of Milo's bed. He fumbles nervously until he pushes both hands into his armpits.

"Remember when you were little, and you cut your hand on the edge of a clay pot?" he asks. "But you were too scared to show me, so you started singing one of your nursery rhymes. I had to beg you to show me your hand so we could take you to get stitches."

Milo nods. "Yeah."

"You're getting too old for me to beg anymore," James says. "I just… want to make sure you're not using your faith to hide from what you're feeling about… everything."

Milo bites his lip until it turns purple. James seems to simper, as if amused by the familiar sight of all his son has inherited from him.

"If you cared, you'd spend the night tonight," Milo says.

James seems to soften, head lowering. "I hate to let you down on your birthday, buddy. But that's just not going to happen."

Although he looks as though he doesn't want to, Milo seems to understand.

"Then, I'm not going to show you my hand," he says. "No matter how much it's bleeding."

Milo flashes a look at his father—a challenge he seems to know his father will never win.

As James inches toward the attic door, Olive slips away and hurries back downstairs. He finds her moments later standing in the foyer.

James swipes his coat from the rack, shoving his arms into both sleeves.

Olive passes him his scarf, her eyes moving back up the stairs as if fearful her son's watching or listening to them.

"How'd it go?" she asks carefully.

James shrugs, wrapping his scarf around his neck. "Fine."

Olive glances at him, unconvinced. James seems to recognize her disapproval immediately.

"He wouldn't talk to me."

"It's not just me then," she says.

James shakes his head, as if wishing he could blame her. "No."

"Things have gotten worse since… you know," she says. "I—never know what to say. I'm always afraid I'm going to say the wrong thing."

"Give him time," he says. "He'll come around."

James starts to head for the door.

Olive bites her fingers. Then, suddenly blurts out: "Hey."

James turns, surprised at first.

"Why don't you stay the night?" she says.

James seems to hesitate, as if unsure.

"I changed the sheets on the bed in the guest room," Olive says. "Fresh towels in there, too. It's too late to drive home anyway."

James shakes his head, biting his lip again. "I don't think it would be a good—"

"Milo wants you to stay," she reminds him. "You can't say 'no' to him on his birthday."

But, of course, he can.

"I have to," he says.

Just as he's about to head for the door again, Olive chases after him.

"What do you want me to say?" she asks, her voice trembling. "You want me to tell you that I want you to stay over too? That I sleep better when you're around? Is that it—?"

"Olive—"

She clears some of the dampness webbing in the corners of her eyes. "Milo isn't the only one who misses you, you know."

James merely nods, visibly thinking what to say.

"Sometimes it's hard to go to bed alone," she says. "The house gets too big."

James folds his arms, as if it were his final defense.

"I'm having my lawyers draw up some papers to be sent to you tomorrow," he says.

"Yes—?"

"To finalize the divorce," he says. "I really think we should."

Everything around her seems to slow to a gentle hum. Olive's eyes shimmer wet. She clears the catch in her throat.

"You met somebody?"

"No. I haven't met anybody. I just—"

"Don't want to be with me."

"Olive," James says, reaching for her.

Olive pushes past him, opening the front door. An invitation to leave. She straightens, composing herself as best she can.

"Drive safe," she says.

James shoves his hands into his pockets, lowering his head.

He slips past her, skirting down the pathway and toward his car.

Olive slams the door behind him.

Her resolve weakening, she chokes on quiet sobs. Knees buckling, she lowers until she crouches on the floor.

What she doesn't seem to notice is Milo watching her from the balcony near the top of the stairs, observing her without expression.

Later that night, Olive finishes wrapping the half-eaten birthday cake and pushes it inside the refrigerator. She licks the frosting from her fingers.

Suddenly, her ears furrow at a strange noise—something being hammered.

Switching off the lights, she glides from the kitchen and scurries up the stairs until she comes upon the small corridor leading toward the attic door.

She knocks.

"Milo?"

Olive pushes her ear against the door, listening.

There's no response.

She pulls on the door handle. Locked.

Olive knocks again. Then, pushes her ear against the door once more.

Finally, the faint sounds of Milo praying drift through the hall and seem to fill the entire house. This time, however, his voice sounds different, as if he were a dying species and issuing a final call to the wild—a final call for help, to be saved, to be rescued, to be permanently absolved.

———

The next morning, light streams in through the kitchen windows. Olive smears strawberry jam across a slice of freshly burnt toast. Eggs sizzle on the stovetop while opera music softly plays from the old record player that they keep in the corner of the dining room.

Olive turns down the gas, grabs the nearby pan, and ladles the eggs onto a small dish. Then, she goes to the kitchen archway and hollers up the stairs, "Milo. Breakfast."

Returning to the kitchen counter, she grabs an avocado from the basket. Then, reaches for the wooden knife block.

It's empty.

Her face scrunches, wondering where she could have misplaced her knife.

Just then, a vulgar thud from upstairs.

Her eyes widen, imagining the worst.

Hurrying up the stairs, she approaches the door leading to the attic.

"Milo—?"

Olive tries the door handle. Still locked.

"Milo, open the door," she orders.

There's no response.

"Milo—?"

Another thud. This one, louder.

Olive steps away for a moment. Then returns with a small screwdriver. She shoves the screwdriver into the lock, twisting it.

The door creaks open.

Olive inches into her son's bedroom, her whole body stiffening.

Suddenly, her eyes widen. Face flushes with terror.

She covers her mouth at the gruesome sight—

A crucifixion.

Milo, dressed only in a pair of white briefs, splayed out against the giant crucifix. His hands—nailed to the cross. His abdomen—slashed and leaking blood as black as oil. His head—lowered as if in silent prayer.

Olive covers her mouth, knees buckling as she staggers back.

She screams and goes on screaming until the paramedics finally arrive. Police cruisers, lights flashing, sit idling in the driveway. An ambulance comes to a halt, siren wailing. When she peers from the window, she notices how neighbors have already gathered on the sidewalk to observe as medics unload a gurney from the rear of the vehicle.

It isn't long before James arrives, swaddling Olive in his arms as she sobs uncontrollably. Meanwhile, officers meander in and out of the house, collecting evidence. Olive shudders, howling like a wounded animal.

An officer approaches James and Olive as they sit on a small sofa arranged in the vestibule. Olive buries her face in James's shoulder as he approaches. The officer passes a small envelope to James.

"We found this among his possessions," the officer explains. Then he moves away.

Olive glances at the envelope and notices it's been addressed to "Mom and Dad" in Milo's handwriting. Together, they unfold the paper and scan the contents. Olive notices James's lips quivering as he reads. Tears bead in the corners of his eyes.

He crumples the letter, burying his face in Olive's hair as she continues to sob.

She turns away as medics pass them, ferrying Milo's lifeless body from the house—taking with them all the joy, all the love, all the familiarity they would ever know, leaving nothing in its place.

THREE

Sunlight shimmers across the surface, sparkling as if the seawater was filled with diamonds.

A small steamboat powers across the channel, a mere speck floating along the horizon.

Its engine sputters, waves parting as it hammers ahead toward a small collection of islands in the distance.

James, dressed in the brand-new summer clothing Olive purchased for him last week, paces back and forth along the boat's narrow deck. He scratches his newly grown beard that Olive continues to complain about.

What does she care anyway? he thinks to himself. *People can't stay the same forever.*

Across the water, he spots a sea otter basking in the morning sun. Snatching the camera dangling from around his neck, James aims it at the small creature and snaps a picture. He lifts his eyes and spots an albatross sailing along a gust of wind, the bird's body washed in golden light.

As the steamboat glides into port, handlers leap from

the bow and onto the dock to secure the rigging. One of the stewards releases the gangplank, the boat finally coming to a full stop.

James scales the platform, descending from the boat and landing on the dock where he's greeted by an overweight man in a tweed jacket.

"Mr. Thornton—?" the man asks.

James tosses his backpack over his shoulders, extending his hand. "Yes. Mr. Patel—?"

They shake hands. James hesitates, surprised by the strength of Mr. Patel's grip.

"Delighted to have you here," Mr. Patel says. "Welcome to Temple Island. How was your ride out?"

"Fine. Fine," James says, narrowly avoiding one of the stewards as they push past him with more rigging from the boat. "They picked me up in Portsmouth. No issues whatsoever."

"Excellent. I knew you'd have no trouble. Like something to eat for breakfast? Our kitchen staff is still serving."

"I think it's best I see the grounds first and get acquainted with everything," James says. "That way I can make it back to the mainland for the two-thirty pick-up."

"Yes. Of course," Mr. Patel says, leading him further up the dock and away from the stewards. "I forgot you're on a tight schedule."

He seems to notice James struggling to secure his backpack.

"Need help with your bags?"

James pulls the backpack tighter over his shoulders. "No. Thank you. I can manage."

James hurries after Mr. Patel as they make their way up the narrow causeway toward the island's main centerpiece—The Enchantment Hotel.

Framed against the lily-white skyline, The Enchantment Hotel rises into view as if it were the discarded remnants of a prehistoric beast.

James and Mr. Patel are mere insects crawling beside the island's monstrosity—from the gables extending from the crimson pitched roof to the broadness of the covered porch wrapping around the entire building.

As they circle the hotel's porch, workers scurry past them carrying large trunks toward the dock.

"We're proud to say we are a totally self-sufficient ecosystem out here," Mr. Patel explains. "All of the island's electricity is powered by solar panels arranged near the harbor."

James aims his camera at the empty rocking chairs lining the hotel's front porch and snaps a picture. "So, you're totally off the grid?"

"Totally. We even hire a seasonal fisherman to catch most of the food we serve to our guests. I hope you and your—" He stops short, stammering as if unsure. "I forget, did you say you were married?"

James, distracted by the hotel, lowers his camera and suddenly realizes it's taken him an uncomfortably long time to answer such a simple question.

"Yes. I am."

"I hope you and your wife enjoy lobster," Mr. Patel says, guiding James further down the path and away from the hotel. "Because chances are that's what you'll be eating most nights."

"She'll be thrilled."

A few yards further down the path and they come upon the island's makeshift lab—a small hovel filled with large glass tanks of various fish and other aquatic life native to the New Hampshire coast.

College-age students crowd around the room's largest tank, spooning lobsters into a bucket.

"This is our marine lab," Mr. Patel explains, steering him inside. "In the summer, we house the science department from the university on the mainland."

James watches as the students collect more lobsters from the tank and deposit them in the bucket.

"What are they doing?" he asks.

"Returning them to the wild. Everything we catch to be studied has to be returned at the end of the summer."

It's then that James makes eye contact with a young woman near the fish tank. He smiles politely at her, but soon realizes that his gaze haslingered for far too long.

"Mr. Thornton. This way."

James's eyes snap to Mr. Patel, who's already holding the door open for him. Embarrassed, he trots past the large man through the open door.

It's not long before Mr. Patel and James come upon a small bungalow tucked on the outskirts of the island—a small Dutch Colonial with painted white shutters.

They tighten their collars as they meander toward the cottage, the salty brine of ocean wind beating hard against them.

"And this is where you and your wife will be staying during your time out here," Mr. Patel explains.

James aims his camera at the tiny house, snapping a picture.

Mr. Patel fishes in his pocket for keys. Finally, he retrieves them.

He ducks beneath the cottage's awning, slips the keys inside the lock. Opens the door.

James inches into a sparsely decorated living room. Antique-looking furniture. No paintings on the walls.

Mr. Patel seems to notice James's unmistakable look of bewilderment.

"You'll have all the creature comforts," he says, as if to put him at ease, if only for a moment.

Mr. Patel sails across the room, flinging open the large windows overlooking the harbor.

"Not to mention, a gorgeous view of the bay," he says.

James scans the room, cautious as if afraid to touch anything. He slides his hand into his pocket and retrieves his cellphone. Fingers flicking across the keyboard, he taps on the screen.

"Wi-Fi?" James frowns at his cellphone. "I don't have much of a signal."

He notices how Mr. Patel's mouth seems to tighten as if he had been hoping he might not ask.

"The luxuries out here are... quite primitive," Mr. Patel says.

"Scary to think of running water as a luxury." James stops himself, imagining the worst. "There is running water, isn't there?"

"Yes. Of course. You won't need cellphones out here," Mr. Patel assures him. "There's a radio outside in the shed that the previous tenants used to coordinate with the coast guard."

James shrugs. *It's not much, but it's something*, he thinks to himself.

"Seems like the perfect place to… escape from everything," he says, meandering toward the large window that looks out over the harbor.

After touring the downstairs, Mr. Patel directs James into the cottage's master bedroom—a modest living space with a queen-sized bed.

James swats at the air, a cloud of dust sparkling in the sunlight. He covers his nose at the rancid smell of antiquity.

Mr. Patel opens the window, a breeze filling the room.

Meanwhile, James studies a large wooden rowing oar pinned to the wall for decoration.

"You think your wife will appreciate the… simple accommodations?" Mr. Patel asks him.

James slides his index finger along the nightstand, revealing a thick coating of grime. "She's been looking forward to it, actually. Plus, I can spend my free time working on my photography."

James ambles toward the bedroom window, looking out at the view.

He spots a smaller island nearby—a narrow strip of land with a small cottage arranged near one of the bluffs. Snaps a photo.

"What's that island called over there?" he asks.

Mr. Patel stands beside James, his eyes following James's index finger as he points. "That's York Island. You won't be allowed over there. Private property. Probably wouldn't want to go there anyhow."

"Why's that?"

"Some of the workers say it's haunted," Mr. Patel says, shoving his hands in both pockets.

"Is it—?"

"Can't say. Never set foot on the island, myself."

"What do they say about it—?" James asks, leaning closer.

"Back before The Enchantment was built, they had some—misfortune—over there," Mr. Patel explains. "A young couple from the mainland had moved to the island. Didn't last long there. Maybe two, three months at the most. Then, one day they vanished. That was it. Never saw them again. It was as if they were never really there. Some of the locals think they were killed by a drifter. Some say their ghosts still walk the island to this very day."

James bites his lip. "Well, not anymore," he says. "Now that they proved—you know. None of it's real."

"Doesn't mean ghosts aren't real," Mr. Patel says.

James senses a gentle breeze whispering all around him as if it were an invitation—a tender beckoning to someone, something he can't quite yet understand.

FOUR

Olive folds a blouse and stuffs it inside a suitcase. She sniffles, choking back quiet sobs as she packs.

A small black cat circles her feet, purring.

Olive swipes a glass of red wine from the nightstand and downs the rest of it. Then resumes packing.

She opens her bureau drawer, digs deep down, and uncovers a crumpled note.

Her eyes go over the words written in Milo's cursive lettering again and again.

She reads, *"If you and Dad love me as much as you say you do, you'll stay together after this. You'll promise me that you'll stay together. No matter what."*

Olive crumples the note, tears welling in her eyes.

Suddenly, her ears pin at the sound of the apartment front door swinging open.

"Olive," James calls out to her from the other room.

Olive shoves the letter inside the drawer, piling clothing on top. She wipes the tears from her eyes, pinching her cheeks.

"In here."

James creeps into the bedroom like an unwelcome house guest. The cat scampers out as soon as he arrives.

Olive hesitates slightly at the sight of him, unsure how to properly greet her husband. As usual, James makes the first move. He leans in, pecking her forehead with a clearly uncomfortable kiss.

"How was it?" she asks him.

"Fine," he says, loosening his tie.

"What did they say?"

"They want me to start in two weeks."

"You got the job?"

James merely nods, sitting on the edge of the bed as he kicks off his loafers and pushes them underneath a nearby chair.

Olive suddenly wraps her arms around him. Then releases him, as if realizing she's overstepped some invisible agreement they've silently arranged.

"I'm so proud of you," she says. "What was it like? What did they say?"

"It wasn't like a normal interview," James explains. "It was almost as if they were waiting for me to turn them down."

"The entire winter. All expenses paid?"

"I have to warn you," he says, swallowing hard. "The accommodations are… sparse."

"You know I don't care about that," she says. "As long as we're together."

But suddenly Olive's smile begins to fade, fear wrapping its fingers around her throat.

"You still want me to come. Don't you?"

But James looks as though he's far away, distant and dreaming.

Olive leans in closer to him, begging for his attention.

"Hey," she says, tenderly taking his hands in hers.

"Sorry."

"You're not thinking of going there without me?" Olive asks, shrinking from him as if afraid of the answer. "Are you?"

"Of course not," James assures her. "You know I'd never."

But Olive can't be convinced.

"You're not thinking of leaving again—?" she asks him.

"How can you say that? You know I'm always going to be here."

Olive shakes her head. "No. You're thinking of leaving again. I can tell."

"What—?"

Olive lowers herself until she's curled on the ground, wringing her hands and panting like a feral animal in heat.

"You're leaving," she whispers. "You only came back to get your things and go."

James crouches beside his wife, wrapping an arm around her. "Darling, you know I'm not going to leave you. I promised you. Didn't I? Didn't I make a promise to you?"

Olive thinks for a moment. "Yes."

"What did I promise you?"

"That you'd never leave again," she says.

"And it's a promise I intend to keep," James tells her.

Olive's breathing begins to steady. She softens, relaxing.

"Now, will you come live with me on a giant rock in the middle of the Atlantic?" he asks her, chuckling slightly.

Olive laughs. For the first time in what feels like a while.

"Yes," she says.

James pecks his wife's head with another kiss. Then, he's on his feet in a matter of seconds.

"That's what I like to hear."

Olive pulls on his sleeve as if she were just a child. "Will you pray with me?"

James shrinks from her. The look on his face—it's a familiar one to Olive. It seems to scream,"Why did she have to ask?"

"Olive," he says gently.

But before he can say anything else, Olive is on her knees at his feet, hands cupped like an encaustic portrait of a penitent sinner.

"Please," she begs him.

Releasing a heavy breath, James kneels beside his wife. Cups his hands and bows his head.

Olive smiles. For the first time, she feels safe. She knows he'd do anything for her, and she quietly wonders to herself what else she can pry from him, what other wealth of wonders she can rob from him to temper her own miserable grief.

FIVE

James braces himself against the bow of the vessel, aiming his camera at the island ahead.

Olive sits nearby, outfitted in a bright red raincoat and holding a small cat carrier with Shayku curled inside.

Rain beats hard against them.

The small vessel steers into the harbor, gliding past the dock where several hotel workers have gathered under umbrellas to wait.

The horn blasts—a spectacular arrival.

James and Olive descend the steps, hauling their suitcases.

A small crowd of hotel workers greet them as they arrive on the dock. Once James and Olive have disembarked, the small crowd begins to funnel onto the boat.

As the crowd parts, James and Olive are greeted by Mr. Patel. He's flanked by two young men who immediately approach them with umbrellas.

"Mr. and Mrs. Thornton," Mr. Patel says. "Beautiful island weather, isn't it?"

The young men snatch the suitcases from James and Olive.

But Olive resists when one of the boys tries to wrench the cat carrier from her hands.

"Shall we?" Mr. Patel says.

James and Olive follow him as he springs further up the dock, following the narrow pathway leading toward the hotel.

The young men toting the bags are not far behind, hoods pulled over their heads as rain pummels them.

They arrive at the small cottage on the outskirts of the island.

The door flings open and Mr. Patel glides into the little house, James and Olive shadowing him.

"Your home away from home," Mr. Patel says.

Olive's eyes scour the room for a semblance of charm. There's none to be had. She frowns.

The two young men arrive, dragging the suitcases.

"Right there is fine, boys," Mr. Patel orders.

Mr. Patel flicks on the light switch. But no light.

The power's out.

James and Olive look at one another in disbelief. *This can't be happening*, they seem to say to one another in the secret language they've invented in the years they've been married.

Mr. Patel laughs nervously. "Fuse must've blown. Billy, go outside to the shed and turn on the generator, will you?"

The young man nods, hastening out of the house. The other follows him close behind.

Mr. Patel hesitates, visibly unsure as he smears the

rainwater from his brow. "We'll have you up and running in no time at all."

"You said we'd have electricity and running water here," James says, folding his arms.

"The water will be pumped in. No trouble there. But the electricity seems to be out for the time being."

Olive begins to pace like a cornered animal and seems to hope that James might take notice.

"There should be enough gas in the generator until the ferryman comes next week with more provisions," Mr. Patel says, skirting into the kitchen with all the craftsmanship of an expert showman. "Until then, we have you stocked up on everything you could possibly need."

He swipes at a box of rat poison from the top shelf. "Even things you may not be thinking about."

James and Olive recoil, bewildered.

"You'll definitely need this in the winter months," Mr. Patel says. "The little pests can be quite the nuisance out here. We have a yearly supply stocked in the hotel as well."

Mr. Patel turns, about to leave, when he suddenly remembers—

"Oh. A word of warning. Careful with the gas stovetop. The dial's broken. Sometimes you think it's off when it's really not."

The lights suddenly flicker on, the generator humming outside.

"And with the flick of a switch, all our troubles disappear," he says.

But Olive glances at James, unconvinced. Their troubles are far from completely disappearing, and she knew that full well.

"Island life isn't for everyone, you know?" Mr. Patel says to them.

Of course, Olive knew this too. But perhaps she hadn't considered the seriousness of her husband's post until they were actually here, until the saltwater of the sea air swept over their skin. There's a small, quiet part of Olive hopeful that James might accept Mr. Patel's life preserver. Then, of course, there's the other part of her that knows full well they need to do this—they need to suffer together or else they'll never be complete without their beloved Milo.

"We're... excited to make it work," James says to Mr. Patel.

It's then Olive glances down and notices a small black beetle crawling at her feet—the only visitor she thinks they'll ever receive in their new home.

Later that same night, Olive serves James a bowl of seafood chowder for dinner, a thin slice of freshly baked bread on the side of the dish.

She watches James as he eyes the soup. Notices him wince, frowning as a shrimp's tail curls at him from the broth.

She recognizes him force the politest smile he can imitate.

"Looks... delicious," he says, swiping a nearby spoon.

Olive, of course, isn't convinced. She sets a bowl down at the table for herself. Sits at the table. Bows her head.

"Bless us, Oh Lord, and these thy gifts which we are about to receive from thy bounty, through Christ, Our Lord. Amen."

After blessing herself, Olive begins to eat.

Out of her peripheral vision, she notices James stirring his spoon in the soup as if pretending to eat. She can't be bothered with his pickiness right now.

"I thought we'd cook the lobster tomorrow afternoon," she says.

"If it's not raining. How many did they leave us—?"

"Enough for the week."

"Be sure to write up a list of things we need for when the ferryman comes next," he tells her.

"We need more bread."

"Already—?"

"They didn't leave us much."

Olive shovels a spoonful of soup into her mouth. Her face suddenly sours. James is right. It tastes as bad as it looks.

She takes a drink of water.

Uncomfortable silence settles over the dinner table.

Olive's eyes lower to her food.

She notices James looking at her, as if hopeful she'll say something.

But she doesn't.

James stirs in his chair. "Do you ever—?"

Olive's attention immediately snaps to him. "Yes?"

But James deflates almost instantly. "Forget it."

"No. What?"

"It was a stupid question," James says, shaking his head.

"What was it—?"

James thinks for a moment. "With everything going on— what they're saying in the news… Do you ever—? I mean, would you…? Have you ever thought of ending things?"

"Between us?"

"Permanently ending things," he says grimly. "For you."

Olive swallows hard, unsure what to say. "You mean, have I ever thought of—?"

But James seems to be unable to even bear the word. "Yes," he says. "After Milo."

Olive senses her skin hardening. "It's a sin in God's eyes."

"Yes. But after what they've said—what they've proved."

"They haven't proved anything. It's not real."

"That's what they're saying."

"They're wrong," Olive tells him. "We'll be reunited with Milo again one day. I know it."

"Isn't it a sin—?"

Olive hesitates for a moment. "Yes?"

"What Milo did."

Olive senses her face heating red, her whole body tensing. "Milo didn't do anything wrong. He was called to God."

James shakes his head, as if in disbelief. "He wasn't called to God, Olive."

"He answered a divine message—a sacred honor to serve in heaven," she says.

"He killed himself."

Without warning, Olive slams her silverware down on the table, leaping out of her seat.

"No, he didn't," she says. "Our son didn't kill himself. God called him because it was time for him to go home. Just like one day it will be ours, too. And on that day, we'll see him again. I know we will. And you can get mad at me and tell me I'm crazy, but you might as well be screaming into the wind of a summer storm. Go ahead. Scream until you're hoarse. Because you know how a storm always answers?

With thunder. I'm not going to be standing next to you when the lightning strikes."

Olive waits for a response from James. But he says nothing.

"I'm not hungry," she says.

Olive rushes out of the kitchen and up the stairs. What she doesn't seem to notice is how the gas dial for the stovetop has been left on, gas hissing as it leaks into the air.

SIX

When James finally gathers the courage to seek out Olive, he finds her dressed for bed and sitting in front of the vanity arranged in the corner of the master bedroom. He watches as she slowly removes her earrings, as if they were somehow miniature replicas of the sadness eating away at her from the inside.

Her eyes snap to him in the mirror. Of course, she turns away.

"You left the gas on," he says. "I turned it off."

But Olive says nothing.

"Look," he says. "I'm sorry."

Olive's eyes rise to meet his in the vanity's reflection.

"I shouldn't have asked."

"Yes," Olive says.

"I shouldn't have said anything."

James rests his hands on Olive's shoulders. "Forgive me—?"

Olive doesn't make him wait as he had expected. She presses one of his fingers against her lips.

James answers her, his hands sliding across his wife's shoulders. Then, down to her waist.

"What if we—?"

"You want to?" she asks.

James leans down, kissing her.

He hesitates, grabbing her breast and squeezing her as he runs his mouth along her forehead.

"I want to," she says, panting in his ear.

"Yes—?"

"I want to have another baby with you," she says.

James suddenly jerks away, his lips pulling downward. "What did you say?"

"Don't you—?"

James stammers, unsure. "I thought we talked about… We decided…"

"I know what we said," Olive says. "But things can change. Can't they—?"

James' eyes lower. "You know I can't… do that anymore."

"I believe in miracles," Olive says, pulling at him gently as if it were a final plea for him to take her, ravage her.

James sits on the edge of the bed. He notices how his wife seems to deflate, her head lowering as if suddenly realizing something unavoidable, something inevitable.

"You don't want to, do you—?" she says.

Just as James is about to open his mouth to speak, there's a loud knock on the door downstairs.

James and Olive look at one another with bewilderment.

"Who could that be—?" Olive asks. "I thought everyone left."

James eyes the wooden rowing oar pinned to the wall: his only defense.

He snatches it and prepares to use it as he creeps out of the bedroom and down the stairs.

James approaches the small entryway, leading the way with the wooden oar. Olive shadows him.

Another forceful knock.

James flicks on the porch light. Then peers out the window at the top of the door.

"Who is it?" Olive asks, buttoning her nightgown and leaning against the bannister for support.

James opens the door, revealing—

A young man in his early twenties.

The young man appears somewhat androgynous—like a model from an Italian Renaissance fresco.

He's outfitted in a black raincoat. Completely drenched. He carries a small, monogrammed black bag.

James lowers the oar, sensing Olive peering out from behind him.

"Yes?" James says.

"I'm sorry," the young man says. "I—saw the lights on in the house and I thought—you could help me."

"What's happened—?"

"I can't make it back to the mainland," the young man says, smearing his hand across his face and wiping away the rainwater. "Do you mind if I—?"

"Yes. Of course, dear," Olive says, ushering him over the threshold and toward the fireplace still smoldering with burned embers. "Come in. You must be freezing."

"Thank you," he says, shaking his sleeves like a dog rescued from a monsoon.

"Here," Olive says, sitting. "Sit by the fire and warm up. Were you sailing in this awful weather?"

The young man glances at his wristwatch. "Left Portsmouth about two hours ago."

James circles his houseguest, his eyes never leaving him. "Horrible day to sail. Have you been sailing long—?"

"Since I was very little," the young man says. "My mom used to pay for lessons."

"And you have your own boat?" James asks, sitting in a nearby chair.

"Yes. I anchored it down near the docks. I thought maybe the hotel would still be open."

"They closed up today."

"We're the winter caretakers," Olive says. "I'm Olive. This is my husband, James."

"I'm sorry to barge in like this," the young man says. "I just—I didn't know where else to go."

"You're lucky you didn't drown out there," Olive says quietly.

James's eyes narrow at their guest. "Yes. I'm surprised such an experienced sailor would go out in this kind of weather."

"Well, I had to," the young man explains. "I felt 'myself growing grim about the mouth.'"

James and Olive look at one another, a soundless question shared between them.

The young man straightens in his chair. "I found 'myself involuntarily pausing before coffin warehouses and bringing up the rear of every funeral I met.'"

James and Olive stare at him, unblinkingly. Unsure.

"You don't know your Melville," the young man says. "It's a line from *Moby Dick*. Captain Ahab takes to the ship every time he feels—troubled... Well, I felt troubled today. And I figured it was high time to get to the sea before I started knocking people's hats off their heads. You see, I have good reason to be troubled."

James leans forward in his chair. "Why's that?"

"My mother died yesterday," the young man says.

Just then, James notices his wife shudder, as if an invisible dagger were twisting in her gut—as if she and the young man were siblings of a similar sorrow.

"Oh. You poor thing," Olive says.

James' head lowers. "I'm... very sorry to hear that."

"I expected you to be distressed considering you knew her," the young man says.

James looks at Olive, as if for an explanation. "I—knew her?"

"Yes... Very well."

The young man fishes inside his coat pocket and produces a small Polaroid picture. He passes it to James.

It's a picture of James—twenty years younger, though unmistakably him—at the hospital bedside of a beautiful young woman as she holds a newborn wrapped in blankets.

Color drains from James' face at the recognition. His voice thins to a whisper. "Where did you get this?"

"My mother gave it to me," the young man says.

"What is it?" Olive asks.

James shoves the picture back at the young man, hiding it from his wife.

"I think it's time to head back to the dock," he says. "The weather should be clearing up."

Before James can intervene, the young man passes the small picture to Olive. "It's a picture of my mother—and your husband."

Olive pales as her eyes scan the Polaroid, realizing.

"Yes," she whispers.

"That was taken the day I was born," the young man explains.

James snatches the photo from Olive, tossing it back to the young man.

"What do you want?" James asks him.

"To find you," the young man says, staring at James.

"So. You found me."

"Yes."

James climbs out of his seat, heading toward the door. "I think it's time for you to leave."

"James. He'll drown if he goes back out there," Olive says, leaping out of her chair. "We have to let him stay."

"Stay?"

"At least until morning when the weather clears," Olive says.

"You're fine to let this... perfect stranger stay with us?"

"He's not a perfect stranger," Olive says. "That picture says otherwise. Doesn't it?"

James' lips tighten, at a loss of what to say.

Olive turns, addressing the young man. "You're more than welcome to stay, dear. I'll take you upstairs to the guest room."

"I don't mean to impose," the young man says.

"It's no trouble at all," Olive says, eyeing her husband. "Right, darling?"

James swallows hard. Reluctant to even speak.

"No trouble," he says quietly.

Olive heads toward the stairs. "Follow me, dear. I'll get you settled."

The young man follows, and they disappear up the stairwell until James is left alone standing beside the fireplace, light flickering against the wall.

SEVEN

After getting their guest settled, Olive returns to the bedroom and finds her husband sitting on the bed and clicking through his camera. She notices him glance at her as if silently begging for an argument.

"You're mad," James says to her.

"I'm not mad."

"I lied to you," he says.

"You told me you were married before," Olive says. "You just never said—"

"—she had a child."

"Yes."

"She got married again not long after we... I never thought... I don't know how he... What are we going to do—?"

Olive looks at James, incredulous. "Going to do? What's to be done?"

"Something has to be," he says.

"He's your son. You owe it to him—"

"Owe what to him?"

"This could be a chance for you—a chance for us—to do things over again," Olive says gently.

James bites his lip, thinking. "He wants money. Why else would he be here?"

"He wants a father."

"I want him gone first thing tomorrow morning," James says, turning over on his side and facing away from Olive.

She merely shakes her head. "You'll get what you want, J. You'll end up all alone on an island you've built for yourself."

Before he can say anything, Olive slips out of the room and leaves him there with nothing more than the sound of the wind rattling the shutters.

Olive finds the young man, undressed down to a white shirt and a pair of underwear, sitting in front of the guest room's vanity. For a moment, she admires him.

She watches as he peels back his collar, scratching his shoulder. Then, he pulls on something.

Olive leans closer, squinting. She can barely make it out: *What is it?*

It looks like—a small feather sticking out of his shoulder.

The young man spies Olive in the mirror's reflection.

Olive flushes, panicked, and recovers as quickly as she can.

"I thought I... Do you—have everything you need—?"

"Yes," he says. "Thank you for the fresh towels."

Olive looks around at the sparsely decorated room. "I—certainly never thought we'd need to use this room."

"Yes," he says. "Why would you expect guests in the middle of the ocean?"

"This is where our son would've slept—if he were with us."

"Did you leave him on the mainland?" the young man asks.

Olive's head lowers. Her voice—brittle and thin. "No... He—passed. Six months ago."

"I'm sorry to hear that," the young man says.

"How did your mother—? If you don't mind my asking."

"She had been sick for a while," the young man explains. "I nursed her as best I could. But a son is a poor replacement for a partner. Just like a mother is a poor replacement for a father... She had spread her message. And when she was finished, God called her to Him."

Olive finds herself staring at the young man, as if bewitched.

"How did your son—? If I may."

"He was—sick, too. I suppose," Olive says. "I didn't realize until it was too late. And then eventually he was... called to God."

"He shared his message with the world," the young man says.

Olive thinks for a moment. She senses herself soften. "Yes. He did."

"What was it—?"

Tears bead in the corners of Olive's eyes. "For—my husband and I to stay together... No matter what."

The young man leans close to Olive. "You see, I believe— no matter what—every human life serves a purpose. We're all messengers. His messengers."

Olive's eyes widen, transfixed. She's in delirium. "Yes. Messengers."

Just then, the tether between Olive and the young man separates, the spell breaking.

"Well, I should let you rest," Olive says, inching toward the door. "Just shout if you need anything."

The young man nods.

Olive's lips crease with a half-smile.

As she moves toward the door, she notices the young man's monogrammed bag leaning against the bedpost.

Her eyes narrow, reading the lettering printed along the bag. The word, "SERAPH."

She squints, puzzled, and then notices the young man staring.

She flashes him a smile. Then skirts out of the room, closing the door behind her.

EIGHT

The next day, James, Olive, and the young man—all bundled in their raincoats—make the trek down the pathway toward the small port. In the distance, they notice a curtain of fog hanging over the harbor.

As they near the dock, Olive notices the young man's face scrunch.

His boat isn't there.

Panic soon sets in.

"Where is it?" he asks.

He races to the end of the pier and locates a seaweed-slimed rope dangling from a wooden post. James and Olive are at his side in a matter of seconds.

"This is where you left it?" James asks him.

"Yes. Tied it up right here."

"Maybe the storm swept it out to sea," Olive says, her head swiveling in every direction.

James folds his arms. "That's just fucking perfect."

"James. You're not helping," Olive says.

"What's he going to do?" James asks her. "He can't swim back to the mainland. It's ten miles away."

"He'll stay with us," Olive tells him.

"You must be joking."

"We have enough food and supplies to tide the three of us over for a week. He can catch a ride with the ferryman when he comes next week to bring more provisions."

"Really. I don't expect you to take me in," the young man says.

"It's no trouble at all," Olive assures him.

"No trouble at all," James says mockingly.

Before he can embarrass himself any further, Olive pulls her husband aside and out of the young man's earshot.

"James. This is your son," she says. "You can't turn your back on him. Do you understand?"

James seems to relax, giving in. He draws in a labored breath.

"We'd... be happy to have you for the week," he says to the young man.

The young man smiles. "That's very kind of you both."

"Come on," Olive says, steering him further up the pathway and away from the dock. "I'll make us some lobster for lunch."

When she glances back to make certain James is following them, she notices him standing at the edge of the dock and gazing out at endless seawater stretching in every direction.

———

Later that afternoon, Olive finds the young man perched on a large rock overlooking the harbor. Rain gently drizzles, the wind murmuring.

The young man leans against a large boulder, his hands shoved in his pockets.

Eyes closed, he recites a prayer in Latin. While he prays, Olive gently approaches him and listens. She pulls her hood to cover her face as a gust of wind slams against her.

When he finishes, he turns and notices Olive staring at him.

"Sorry," he says. "I thought I was alone."

"You know Latin?" she asks him.

"Some. My mother taught me."

Olive's mouth opens with muted words at first. There's something she's been aching to tell him—something that's been circling inside her mind since they had first met.

"He doesn't have much money," she tells him.

"What?"

"We did. Once," she explains. "But most of it is gone now. If that's what you're after."

The young man shrinks, offended. "That's not why I'm here."

"I didn't know if you—"

"No," he assures her. "It's not. It never was."

Silence falls over them for a moment.

Olive stares out at the ocean, the breeze murmuring all around her.

"What do you want?" she asks him.

The young man frowns. Lowers his head, as if afraid she would eventually ask.

"I'm here to share a message," he says.

Olive senses herself loosen, glacial remnants buried deep inside her suddenly thawing. "Yes?"

"But. It's one I'm not ready to share yet," he says.

Olive merely searches his face for an explanation.

She glances heavenward and notices more clouds gathering overhead, as if the hand of God were curtaining the entire world.

NINE

Later that evening, Olive finds James undressing in the bedroom. She slams the door shut behind her, startling him.

"What's the word people say when they find something they've been looking for?"

"Eureka," he says.

"Yes. Eureka."

"You've found something?" he asks her.

"I've come to a realization," she says.

"Yes?"

"Something you're not going to believe. Something you're going to tell me I'm crazy for thinking. But I need you just this once to hear me out. Beliefs are like bugs on flypaper. You know what I'm saying? They're hard to shake off."

James straightens. Hesitant, but seemingly willing to listen. "OK. You have my attention."

"I—don't think he's your son," she says.

"You saw the picture."

"I saw the picture," she says. "But I still don't think he's your son."

206

"Who do you think he is—?"

Olive stares at James. *He'll never believe me*, she thinks to herself.

"There's just—something about him."

"Yes—?"

"I think he's something else."

James glares at her. "What—?"

"I think he's an angel," she whispers.

"You can't be serious."

"Listen to me," she says. "He appeared as if out of nowhere."

"His boat was swept away."

"His bag has the word 'Seraph' printed on it."

James shakes his head. "Could be the man his mother married—a last name…"

"He says he's here to share a message," Olive tells him.

James rolls his eyes. "Yes. What a shitty father I've been."

"No," Olive insists. "He's here to tell us something."

"Tell us what?"

Olive closes her eyes and relaxes slightly, as if a warm light were filling her from deep inside. "A message from Milo. We must help him. We have to do whatever we can to make sure he tells us."

James says nothing.

Olive gazes out the bedroom window, watching more thunderstorm clouds drift across the dark sky.

TEN

The following morning, James finds Olive's side of the bed empty. He hears the clatter of pans, the sizzling of eggs on the stovetop, and slowly creeps down the stairs where he finds Olive and their new houseguest in the kitchen. Olive whisks between the refrigerator and the kitchen counter, eggs and strips of bacon cooking. Shayku mills about at her feet, occasionally meowing and tirelessly searching for scraps.

Olive slices fruit, arranging fresh pieces on a plate.

Then, serves it to the young man.

"It looks delicious," he says, warmly.

"Something to drink?" she asks. "Coffee?"

"If you have any juice?"

Olive leans into the refrigerator, pulling out a fresh carton of orange juice.

James does a double take at the amount of food piled on the kitchen table. Fresh eggs, toast, strips of bacon, croissants, pancakes—a feast.

"What's the occasion?" he asks.

Olive looks at him, bewildered. "What do you mean?"

"Did you cook everything in the pantry—?"

James swipes a strip of bacon. But Olive quickly swats him away.

"Those are for our company," she says.

James eyes their house guest as the young man smiles sheepishly at him.

Olive pours a glass of orange juice, setting it in front of the young man.

"I wanted to make sure he was well fed this morning," she says, returning to the stovetop.

James opens the refrigerator door and pales when he sees empty shelves. "Olive..."

"Yes, dear?"

"There's hardly anything in here. Did you cook everything we had—?"

"I wasn't sure what he liked," she tells him.

James can scarcely believe it.

"That was most of our food for the week," he says.

"We'll get more next week when the ferryman arrives," Olive says.

"I told you we have to ration everything now that there's three of us," James tells her. "Just in case."

"Don't worry. It'll be fine."

Not wanting to argue, James takes a deep breath and withdraws from Olive. He approaches the young man seated at the kitchen table.

"I'm going out to the shed to split more wood for the fire," he says. "Like to come and help me?"

Olive pushes herself in between them, sliding another

209

plate of food in front of the young man. "He can't go outside. He hasn't had his breakfast yet. Besides, it's too cold to work out there. He'll get sick."

James rolls his eyes. He grabs his raincoat and heads out the front door, slamming it shut behind him.

James arranges a log on a chopping block. Swings down an axe over his shoulder and chops the wood in half.

He kicks the splintered pieces aside to form a pile near the shed. He swipes another log from the pile and arranges it on the chopping block.

James looks up from his work, peering through the small cottage window.

Framed there, the young man lazes on the couch while Olive kneels in front of him, serving him a tray of tea and freshly baked biscuits.

James raises the axe high above his head and slams the blade down against the log, splitting it in half.

Later that night.

James flings open the door to the master bedroom, freezing in his tracks as he finds the young man lounging in the bed.

The young man straightens, pulling sheets to cover himself. He rubs his eyes, as if dazed.

James squints at him. "What are you doing in here—?"

"I—"

Olive suddenly appears in the doorway behind James.

"Darling, I've moved our things," she tells him.

James turns, incredulous. "Moved our things—?"

"I thought our guest would be more comfortable in here," she says warmly. "The other room is too small, after all."

James's hands curl to fists. "Yes. Certainly, too small for two people to share."

"We can sacrifice a little comfort, can't we?" Olive asks. "For the sake of our visitor. We want him to be comfortable, don't we—?"

Olive finishes outfitting the bed in the guest room with new sheets while James undresses.

"You're out of your mind," he says to her, unbuttoning his shirt.

"I knew you'd be upset," she says, shaking her head.

"It's our bedroom and you're letting that brat take over the house."

James notices how Olive's cheeks begin to heat red.

"I didn't think you'd embarrass me like that in front of him," she barks at him.

"Embarrass you? You care what that mealy-mouthed urchin thinks of us?"

Olive stares blankly at her husband for a moment, as if she cannot believe what he's saying. "Urchin? That's what you call him?"

"Yes," James says.

He unbuckles his pants, folding them across a nearby chair. Then, he climbs into bed.

"I told you," she says, "he's a divine being."

James runs his fingers through his hair. "I can't listen to this anymore."

"He has a message for us. He told me himself."

"He's probably going to take a hammer from the shed and use it to split our heads open one night."

"Milo's trying to speak to us through him," Olive says. "I know it…"

James turns over on his side, facing away from his wife.

"Aren't you forgetting something—?"

James peers over his shoulder at her.

"Your prayers," she says.

But James ignores her, rolling over to sleep. He reaches for the lamp on the nightstand, switches off the light.

Olive kneels beside the bed, cupping her hands.

He listens to her as she prays in the darkness.

ELEVEN

The following day.

Olive serves the young man a bowl of hot soup.

She hesitates for a moment.

"How does it look—?"

The young man grabs a spoon, taking a mouthful. "It's delicious."

Olive exhales, relieved. "Good. I—didn't have much left. But I wanted to make sure you liked it."

She's about to sneak back to the stovetop when—

"Hey," the young man says to her.

She turns gently.

"Sit with me—?"

Olive's face flushes, as if she's been asked to dine with royalty.

She shrugs off her apron and sits across from the young man.

Olive's eyes avoid him, nervous, as silence lingers over the table.

"I'm afraid I'm a poor companion for conversation," she says.

"Sometimes words ruin everything."

Olive nods. "I—suppose you're right."

Another painfully long pause.

"If you could have anything in the world, what would you want—?" he asks her.

Olive begins to laugh, nervously. "What a thing to ask…"

"I felt as though you'd answer truthfully," he says.

Olive considers for a moment, as if secretly embarrassed about how long it takes her to answer.

"You're probably expecting me to say I want my son back. That's what any mother would say. Right—?"

"Is that what you want—?"

Olive shakes her head. "No… He was called to God for a reason. How could I question that? No, there's something else I want…"

The young man leans closer to her. "Yes?"

"I'd give anything to have another child to take care of," she tells him, looking off distant and dreaming.

It's not long before she returns to reality.

"But it's out of the question, I'm afraid… James wouldn't want another one now anyway…"

Without warning, Shayku leaps on the table and knocks over the young man's bowl of soup.

The young man lurches back, sneezing violently, as soup splashes all over his shirt and pants.

"Oh, you poor thing," Olive calls out. "I'm so sorry."

She shoos the cat. It scampers away, tail raised.

"Bad Shayku!"

Olive grabs nearby paper towels and dabs the young man's damp shirt.

"Here. This should help."

The young man laughs. "I probably should've mentioned I'm allergic to cats."

"You are—? Oh, I'm so sorry. I'll make sure he stays away from you."

The young man's eyes follow Olive as she dabs his shirt.

"Here. You better come upstairs with me and let me clean those before the stain sets…"

The young man heads for the stairs. He turns when he notices Olive isn't following.

"Are you coming—?" he asks her.

Olive stalls, standing beside the front door.

"You go on up," she tells him. "I'll be there in a minute."

The young man disappears up the stairs.

When he's out of sight, Olive begins the hunt. She cranes her head beneath end tables, sofas, etc. Finally, she finds what she's looking for—Shayku.

She snatches him from his hiding place and delivers him to the front door.

She tosses the cat outside on the front porch and slams the door shut.

Olive reaches the master bedroom and finds the young man already shirtless.

She marvels at his sculpted abdominals, the firmness of his pectorals—a perfect specimen of masculinity.

"I tossed the shirt on the bed," he tells her. "Is that OK—?"

Collecting herself, Olive swipes the shirt and admires the stain.

"Yes. I should be able to get this out."

She notices the dark spot blooming from the front of his pants. Clears the catch in her throat to speak.

"Your pants, too," she says. "I can clean those."

The young man unbuckles his belt and slips off his pants, revealing his white underwear.

He passes the soaked pants to Olive, their fingers sliding against each other's.

Olive shudders at his touch as if a spark of electricity were snaking through her entire body.

She draws closer to him, as if she were carefully testing his comfort.

He does not shrink or recoil.

She reaches out to touch his face. He touches hers.

Their bodies are pulled together by an invisible rope and finally they kiss, mouths devouring one another.

Olive rips off her blouse as the young man pushes her down on the bed, mounting her. His hands slide all over her body, his lips pressed against hers.

He pulls away for a moment, Olive's lips pout as he abandons her.

As if enacting some ancient ritual, the young man presses the palm of his hand against her forehead.

Olive rakes her head back, spasming in ecstasy.

Just then, the sound of the door opening downstairs.

They hear James's voice as he calls for his wife.

Olive leaps off the bed, throwing on her blouse.

The young man tosses on his shirt, hoisting his pants around his waist.

Olive and the young man, both flushed, descend the stairs and find James in the vestibule holding Shayku.

"I found him out in the cold, crying," he tells them.

Shayku jumps from his arms, scurrying under the couch.

"Did you let him out by accident?" James asks.

"I've been looking all over for him," Olive says. "Thank you, darling."

Olive scurries into the kitchen, resuming her work.

Out of her peripheral vision, she sees James notice the dark stains on the young man's shirt.

"Accident—?"

"The cat," the young man says. "Spilled on me."

James nods, heading up the stairs and disappearing into the guest bedroom.

Olive and the young man glance at one another.

TWELVE

The following morning.

A gust of ocean wind rattles the scraggly bushes arranged beside the entrance of the cottage. Rain drizzles.

James steps out the front door, holding a cup of coffee.

He pulls his coat's collar around his neck as a breeze whispers all around him.

He glances down and notices something dark lying beneath one of the bushes. He peels back the leaves and then he sees it—

Shayku. Lying there. Dead.

The cat's little corpse—damp and crusted with ice.

That afternoon, James, Olive, and the young man gather around a roaring fire arranged beside one of the boulders overlooking the ocean.

James hurls a small blanket-wrapped bundle onto the pyre.

Olive and the young man respectfully bow their heads.

The clouds begin to darken, plumes of smoke stretching their fingers across the sky.

———

Later that night.

Olive slips on her nightgown while James lounges in bed.

He watches as she stares at herself in the mirror. Then, her eyes glance at him.

"Do you still love me—?" she asks.

James straightens, bewildered by the question. "Still?"

"We haven't… in a while…"

James folds his arms. "You haven't wanted to."

"I haven't wanted to?"

"Yes."

"I've wanted to," she says. "I just didn't realize I need to beg for it."

"You say you have a headache. Or that you're too tired."

A long, uncomfortable pause.

"You probably couldn't even fuck me if you tried," she says to him.

James stares at her, his eyes narrowing to slits. "What was that?"

"You fucking heard me," she says.

Without warning, James rips off the sheets, leaping up. He grabs Olive and tosses her down on the bed, mounting her.

Mouths pressed against one another, Olive shucks off her nightgown as James thrusts against her. Again and again.

For the first time in over a year, they make love. To James, it feels as though they're two affection-starved creatures trying to crawl inside one another.

THIRTEEN

A WEEK LATER

James, Olive, and the young man gather on the dock as a rain shower passes overhead.

They stare out at the empty horizon for what feels like hours. No sign of the ferryman.

James frowns, recognizing the truth: "He's not coming."

He turns, marching back up the pathway toward the hotel.

Olive and the young man are left on the dock, unsure.

Later, James skulks out to the shed behind the house and activates the radio on the workbench.

He presses the button, then speaks into the microphone.

"Hello. James Thornton of Temple Island, here. Do you read me—?"

The radio hisses static at him.

"Hello. I'm calling from Temple Island. Is anybody there—?"

The radio hisses again, screeching this time.

James slams the microphone down on the bench, shutting it off.

The lights in the kitchen are out, the generator in the shed now officially extinct.

Olive lights her way around the area with candles, going from the kitchen faucet to the counter.

She delivers a tray of cold beans to the table where James and the young man are waiting.

James winces, looking down at the pitiful rations set in front of him.

Olive seems to notice his joylessness.

"It's all we have left," she tells him.

James grimaces, digging his spoon into the bowl of beans and eating.

Olive leans over the toilet, vomiting.

She pulls her head out of the bowl, wiping her mouth.

Looks down at her bloated stomach. She rubs it.

She feels something. A kick?

She rises from trembling knees, meeting her reflection in the bathroom mirror.

Her eyes widen. Hopeful.

Olive, dressed in her raincoat, pulls back the sliding wooden door and enters the small shed.

She finds James sitting at his workbench. He's threatening the radio with a screwdriver.

James glances at her. "So. Where is he—?"

Olive's face scrunches, confused.

"Your shadow," he says.

"I have something I need to tell you…"

James laughs, resuming his work. "You found a way off this rock?"

"I think I'm pregnant," she says.

James looks up from his work, suddenly visibly shaken by the mere suggestion.

"You're—?"

"I missed my period last week. And I've been sick almost every day…"

James shakes his head in disbelief. "But, I can't… Anymore…"

"I know…"

"So, how are you—?"

"It's a miracle," she says.

"A miracle—?"

Olive shrinks, suddenly noticing her husband's disgust.

"Are you happy?"

"I just don't… How can you be—?"

"You're not…"

"No. That's not it."

"You don't want me to be pregnant," she says.

Olive turns away, fighting back tears. James grabs her arm, pulling her close to him.

"Hey. Listen. You know I love you more than anything in the world… If you're happy, I'm happy."

"You are—?"

"Yes."

"You're happy?"

James pecks Olive on the forehead with a kiss.

"Very."

He pulls his wife in close for a kiss on the lips.

They remain locked in a permanent embrace.

What they don't seem to notice is the young man observing them from the shed's small doorway.

Olive lazes in bed.

James enters, carrying a serving tray of cold rations. He slides the tray onto his wife's lap.

"Thank you, darling," she says.

"I still haven't been able to get through to the mainland to schedule you a doctor's appointment," he tells her.

She laughs. "I don't suppose they'd do a house call out here."

"I'll try again right now."

James pecks Olive's forehead with a kiss. Then hurries out of the room and down the stairs, where he finds the young man waiting for him.

"Lunch today—?" the young man asks.

"Whatever you can make yourself," James says.

He snatches his raincoat from the rack, tosses it on, and runs out the front door.

That night, James and Olive peer out the window, observing the young man as he wanders out to one of the boulders overlooking the sea to pray.

"He'll be a while," Olive quietly says to her husband.

James fastens the latch on the front door.

Then, James and Olive tiptoe up the stairs and disappear into the guest bedroom.

They don't hear the sounds of the young man pounding on the front door, calling to be let inside.

They're far too busy enraptured with one another's naked bodies. They kiss, mouths devouring one another as James slams his hips against his wife.

Later that night.

Olive sneaks down the stairs, a small candle lighting the way, and heads for the kitchen when she hears a loud knock.

Olive approaches the door, unfastens the latch.

The young man crouches on the porch, shivering.

"I was calling for you," he says.

"We didn't hear," Olive tells him.

"I called your name…"

"I'm sorry…"

Olive withdraws, leaving the door open for the young man.

He straightens, crossing over the threshold and into the house.

FOURTEEN

The following afternoon.

The young man enters the master bedroom and finds Olive arranging her suitcase on the bureau.

"What are you doing—?"

Olive hardly looks at him, busy folding her clothes.

"Reorganizing," she says.

She watches him as he scans the room for his belongings.

"Where are my things—?".

"I moved them back to the guest room."

The young man shakes his head, his mouth hanging open as if unable to comprehend. "You had said I could sleep in here."

"That was before…"

"Before—?"

"The master suite gets better sunlight in the afternoon," Olive says, rubbing her stomach. "That helps baby."

Olive crosses toward him, grabbing the door handle.

"Would you excuse me? I'm due for my nap…"

The young man, speechless, bows out of the room as Olive closes the door in his face.

Another rainy evening. The distant rumble of thunder.

James lies in bed, holding a book close to a small candle for light as he reads.

It's still. Quiet. Peaceful.

Without warning, an ear-splitting howl from the bathroom.

James leaps out of bed, rushing toward the bathroom door.

He tries the handle. It's locked.

"Olive," he says. "Olive, baby. What's wrong?"

Another deafening howl. This one almost sounds inhuman. Hoarse with pain.

James slams his body against the door. The frame buckles.

He slams himself again. And again. Finally—

The door bursts open.

James sails into the bathroom.

Sliding across a puddle of blood, he crashes against the wall.

Steadying his footing, he finds Olive crouching beside the toilet. Blood leaks from between her open legs.

The floor tiles are streaked with red.

James covers his mouth at the sight.

Olive wipes the snot from her nose, sobbing.

"It's—it's gone…"

She lowers her head, choking on sobs.

James peers into the toilet bowl. Grimaces at the gruesome sight. He slams the lid shut.

Then, he wraps his arms around his wife and pulls her off the ground. She trembles as he steers her out of the bathroom and toward the bed.

Days later.

Olive reclines in bed, rolled over on her side. Her eyes are fixed on the wall, far off and daydreaming.

All color has drained from her face.

James knocks on the door, enters.

"Hey," he says.

Olive turns. Looks at him. Then, rolls back over on her side.

"Can I get you anything—?"

Olive breathes quietly. "I'm fine…"

"I'll be outside in the shed. Trying to get the radio to work."

Olive doesn't react.

"Shout if you need anything…"

James slips out of the room, closing the door behind him.

Later that afternoon. Rain drizzles.

James arranges a log on the chopping block. Slams the axe down, splitting the log in half. The pieces skate aside.

The young man approaches him, pulling his hood over his head.

"Need any help—?"

James eyes the young man up and down, as if appraising his willingness to help. Judges him with an "Are you serious?" look.

But the young man doesn't back down.

"Grab those pieces and start a pile over there," James orders him.

The young man bends down, collecting the severed logs.

James places another log on the chopping block, glancing at the young man.

"Why did you come here—?"

The question seems to startle the young man. He blushes, as if unsure how to answer.

"There must be a reason," James says.

A long pause.

"I once heard a story about a son who hated his father," the young man says. "So, do you know what he did? One night, when his father was sleeping, he crept into his room with a bottle of bleach and poured some into his ear. He thought it was finished. Thought his father was dead. But, do you know what happened next? You'll never guess. Imagine the young man's surprise the next morning when his father shows up at the breakfast table, his eyes dimmed and glassy, blood leaking from both ears... Despite being completely braindead, he still went through his morning routine... And you know what I thought when I heard that? I never want that to be me. I never want to merely go through the motions. I want to be free... Don't you want the same—?"

James considers the sentiment for a moment. His lips crease with a smile. He turns, facing the cottage.

He glances through the kitchen window; he spies Olive cleaning the house—the prison they've created.

His eyes return to the young man and it's then he notices something—

The young man bites his lip, thinking. Just like James does.

James relaxes, letting his guard down.

"You missed one," James says, pointing at the ground.

The young man snatches a piece of wood he had missed, gathering a bundle in his arms.

James thaws, watching him arrange the wood in a small pile.

FIFTEEN

Olive, bundled up in her raincoat, sits on one of the large boulders overlooking the ocean.

She looks off, distant.

Her breathing—shallow. Her eyes—swollen from crying.

The young man approaches, startling her.

"Sorry," he says.

Olive looks off again, watching more clouds gather overhead.

"Can I sit—?"

Olive considers for a moment. Then nods gently.

The young man hoists himself up onto the rock.

They sit in peaceful silence for a moment—the only sound the crashing of the waves against the rocks down below.

"Is there anything I can do—to help—?" he asks.

Olive looks at him as if surprised he would ask. Then, merely shakes her head.

"How do you feel—?"

A long, thoughtful pause before Olive finally answers.

"Like a candle burning at both ends," she says. Her head

lowers, lips moving with muted words at first. "I just—never thought…"

But her voice trails off.

"Yes—?"

"I never thought it would happen… And then, it finally did. I loved the way it felt—carrying something, you know? …Now, I feel empty. Like a part of me is gone forever…"

"That which is done is what will be done," the young man says.

Olive swallows hard, turning to the young man.

"If it is His will, then it shall be."

"His will—?"

But the young man doesn't respond. His eyes drift out to the horizon, his expression dimming with peacefulness.

Olive's eyes search him for an explanation. She finds none.

James relaxes in bed, reading a book by candlelight.

Olive creeps into the room, closing the door behind her.

Her voice—a mere whisper. "Did he go to bed—?"

James straightens slightly. "I think so… Where were you—?"

"Out," Olive answers. "I've been thinking."

"Yes—?"

"About him."

"What about—?"

"I think I was wrong," Olive says. "I've been wrong this whole time."

James sits up in bed, setting his book aside. "Finally, you're coming to your senses. What made you decide?"

"I don't know how I could've been so stupid."

James peels back the bedsheets. "Here. Come to bed."

"I can't. We have work to do."

James's face curls in a question. "Work—?"

"Something needs to be done."

"About what—?"

"About him," Olive says.

"What about him—?"

Olive's voice thins to a whisper. "He's not who he says he is…"

"But the picture," James says.

"I'm not talking about the picture. I'm talking about him."

"Yes—?"

"He's not an angel," Olive says. "I thought he was. But I think he's something else… Something horrible…"

James rolls his eyes, folding his arms. "Please, Olive. Not this."

Olive peers over her shoulder, as if someone were listening.

"I think he's a demon—sent to hurt us."

James's eyes widen in visible disgust. "Olive. You can't be serious."

"I know how it sounds. But we have to do something."

"Do something—?"

"He's the reason we lost the baby," she says.

"Olive. Please."

"We can't stay here with him."

"Do you realize what you're saying—?"

"Yes. I know you don't believe me. But I'm begging you to trust me. We have to get rid of him."

James does a double take. "Get rid of him—?"

"If we don't, we'll die... I don't think he was sent here with a message from Milo." She covers her mouth, horrified. "I think he was sent to destroy us."

The sound of footsteps creaking outside in the hallway.

Olive's attention snaps to the door. She spies a dark shadow flickering in the candlelight beneath the doorway.

As suddenly as it appeared, the shadow flits away, vanishing.

The next day.

Rain slows to a mere trickle. The sky—still dim and cloudy.

Olive opens the front door and sprints down the narrow pathway toward the shed. She finds James and the young man busy at work, chopping more wood for the fire.

She startles them.

"Can I see you both in the house—?"

She doesn't wait for them to answer, running back to the house.

James drops the axe, the young man tossing the splintered wood aside as they follow her.

When they've congregated in the living room, James and the young man seated on the couch, Olive stands, addressing them.

She swallows hard, as if about to recite something she had rehearsed. Her voice—wooden, stilted.

"I—think we can all agree that the last few weeks have been—tense. To say the least."

She pauses, waiting for a reaction from James or the young man. Nothing.

"The fact is—the house is too small for three people," she says. "What was initially supposed to be a week of hospitality has turned into over a month."

Olive notices the young man shrink in his seat, as if embarrassed.

"It's not his fault, Olive," James says.

"No. Of course not," Olive says. "I would never dream of accusing anyone. Or saying it's someone's fault... But we need to do something so that we can live out the rest of the winter season—comfortably."

James's eyes flash to the young man. "Aren't you comfortable here—?"

The young man stammers, unsure.

"The three of us can't stay in this house for another month," Olive says firmly. "That's why I'm proposing we relocate him to the empty hotel for the remainder of the season."

James's eyebrows furrow at his wife. "You want to banish him—?"

"You said there are some supplies stored there. He won't go hungry. Enough to last him until the ferryman returns."

"If he returns," James reminds her.

"Guests are going to return to the hotel for the summer season no matter what," Olive says. "Somebody will come for us eventually."

"You want us to break into the hotel?"

"Mr. Patel left you the key."

"For emergencies only," James says. "We're not allowed in there."

"I think this counts as an emergency," she says. "We'll gather his things and take him over there this afternoon."

She glances at the young man. "How does that sound?"

The young man exhales, regarding James. Then, back at Olive. "I suppose that's fine."

"Then. It's settled," she says.

Thinking she's won, Olive begins to move out of the living room when James stops her.

"No," he says.

Olive turns gently. "No?"

"He's not leaving," James says.

"James. We talked about this."

"You act like you're the only person in the world who's ever lost something, someone."

Olive winces, hurt a little. But she won't back down. James seems to recognize this.

"Fine," James says. "If that's how you're going to be. I'll stay at the hotel with him."

Olive's eyes widen at the prospect of being left on her own. "You'd leave me here—?"

"You can come stay with us. Or you can stay here. It's your choice."

Olive considers for a moment. She isn't surprised. In fact, a part of her had always been expecting this.

"If that's the way you want it," she says, folding her arms and walking out of the room.

James and Olive, lugging James's suitcases, climb the rocky pathway leading from the cottage to the hotel's entrance.

The young man, toting his black bag, lags behind.

The ocean wind blasts them as they walk, a monsoon surrounding them.

James points out a large rock in the middle of the pathway.

But Olive's hood suddenly slides down, covering her eyes until she cannot see where she's going.

She takes another step and—

SNAP.

Her ankle twists against a small rock. She lurches forward, screaming.

James and the young man immediately dash to her rescue as she lies on the ground, spasming and screaming in pain.

James kneels beside his wife, comforting her. "Where is it—?"

Olive sobs, pointing to her ankle.

James gently lifts her pant leg, revealing a blood-slimed bone jutting out from her ankle.

"Shit," James says quietly.

"We have to set it," the young man says.

Olive howls in agony, raking her head back.

"Baby, this is going to hurt," James tells her. "But it's going to be over soon. I promise."

Olive shakes her head, as if begging him not to touch her. She chokes on sobs.

James grabs hold of Olive's ankle and with a swift motion, he snaps the bone back into place.

Olive screams until hoarse, her shouting drowned out by a hiss of wind.

SIXTEEN

James and the young man, carrying Olive between them, scale the steps to the hotel's front porch.

Arranging her beside the main entrance, James digs into his pocket and fishes out a small key.

He slides the key into the lock, twisting it. The door opens.

Carrying Olive in his arms, the young man crosses the threshold and enters the hotel's dimly lit lobby.

James follows, closing the door behind him.

Their eyes scour the entryway—from the hotel's front desk to the empty Victorian-styled chairs and sofas nearby.

The young man delivers Olive to one of the couches, tenderly setting her down.

She flinches, her foot still throbbing in agony.

"Go see if you can find some bandages," James orders the young man. "Anything to dress the wound."

He ventures off, disappearing down a dark corridor.

James kneels beside Olive as she lies sprawled out on the sofa.

"J," she gently says to him, tugging on his sleeve.

"Just try to rest," he says.

Olive pulls him closer by the collar, peering over his shoulder to make sure the young man has left.

"He did this to me," she whispers to him.

"Olive."

"He wanted to hurt me."

James throws his hands in the air. "I'm not listening to this."

"If we don't do something, he's going to kill us."

"What would you have me do?" he asks her.

Olive answers him with merely a look—a look that seems to say, "You know what we have to do."

James shrinks a little, unsure. "You're not saying—?"

"It's the only way. He's going to kill us."

"I'm not going to listen to this anymore."

The young man suddenly returns, guiding a small empty wheelchair and carrying a box of candles. "Look what I found."

In the distance, a soft rumble of thunder.

Olive wheels herself into the kitchen. Winces in pain as her bandaged foot knocks against the leg of a small table.

She covers her mouth, stifling a scream.

Composing herself, she moves herself over to the pantry and flings open the doors—shelves stacked with non-perishables.

Olive wheels over to the kitchen sink. Opens the drawer beneath and rummages through the bottles of bleach and dish detergent.

Finally, she locates what she had been looking for—a box of rat poison.

She pours some out on a cutting board. Then, fishes inside a drawer for a large knife.

Olive minces the pellets up until they're a fine powder.

She uncorks a nearby bottle of Cabernet and slides the powder into the bottle, the poison dissolving.

Thunder cracks. Lightning flickers as rain hammers hard against the kitchen windows.

Later, Olive, James, and the young man gather in the hotel's massive dining room and arrange themselves at one of the tables. Candlelight rinses the walls in a shimmering glow.

Several bowls filled with canned stew, a loaf of bread arranged on the side. A few bottles of wine are nearby too—especially the bottle of Cabernet.

James spoons some meat from the stew. Takes a bite.

"We should've come here sooner," he says, his mouth full.

"Will they be upset—?" the young man asks.

Olive stares at the bottle of Cabernet. Then, at the young man.

James shakes his head. "I'll explain to them what happened. We just may not be invited back next year."

"I wouldn't want to come anyway," Olive says quietly, stirring her spoon inside her half-empty bowl.

She grabs the bottle of Cabernet, offering it to the young man.

"Something to drink—?"

The young man nods, covering his mouth.

Olive pours him a glass. Then, hands it to him.

She watches him as he takes a drink. Then, another.

His face scrunches.

"It has—an aftertaste."

"Most Cabernets do," James says, snatching a piece of bread. "Here. Let me try."

With one swift motion, James downs the rest of the glass.

"No," Olive calls out.

She lunges for him, but she's too late.

James pales, looking at his wife.

"What is it—?"

Olive shakes her head, covering her mouth in horror.

"You weren't supposed to—"

But her voice trails off, the words far too unpleasant to utter.

"Weren't supposed to—?"

The realization suddenly creeps across James's face. He stares at the empty wine glass. Then at Olive. He seems to understand.

"Olive," he says gently. "What—have you done—?"

Olive wheels across the table, toward her husband.

James opens his mouth, as if about to vomit.

His eyes roll to the back of his head as he spasms uncontrollably, limbs flailing.

Olive watches as he slides out of his chair, collapsing to the floor and twitching like a dying insect.

He retches, foaming at the mouth.

Olive leaps out of the wheelchair, kneeling beside him.

"No. God, please," she murmurs.

She looks back to the young man only to find—

He's gone.

She scans the dark corners of the room. Squints, thinking she sees something—the thin arm of a giant spider—curling out of the darkness where the two walls meet.

Her attention returns to James as he twitches helplessly.

"J," she says. "Please."

James's breathing slows, his lips drooling with foam.

She pounds on his chest. But he does not respond.

Olive shakes his lifeless body, finally realizing that he's dead.

She buries her face in his chest, sobbing uncontrollably.

Without warning, dark roots sprout from the floor and swaddle her husband's lifeless body.

Olive lurches back, horrified at the sight.

The vines swallow him completely, tendrils curling beneath his skin. His eyes bulge, roots slipping underneath his eyelids and coiling there.

Olive rubs her eyes in disbelief.

As if the floor were inhaling him, James's body shrinks under the tress of whispering roots until he's nothing more than a dark stain.

He vanishes.

Olive presses her fingers against the dark outline of his body seared against the floor.

She wipes the tears from her eyes, sniveling.

Just then, Olive notices something emerge from the darkness surrounding the dining room.

It's Mr. Patel.

But he's completely changed: a vile monstrosity.

His face is gaunt—sunken cheekbones, hollow eye-sockets. His limbs—needle-thin. His skin—practically transparent. His body—the glistening black shell of a beetle.

He crawls on four legs as if he were an insect.

"Olive," he says softly.

Olive's eyes widen as she studies the large creature.

"Follow me," he hisses.

And with that, the monstrosity scurries out of the room and out of sight.

Olive limps after him, dragging her bandaged foot.

She limps out of the dining room and into the dark corridor.

She slows as she scans the narrow hallway—the walls teeming with faceless human bodies bulging from the woodwork.

A grotesque puzzle of human anatomy.

Their skeletal limbs ironed into the wood, coiled with roots, as if they were in the process of dissolving into the walls.

They moan as Olive passes them, caught in their exquisite form of bondage.

She nears the end of the hallway and arrives at the empty hotel lobby.

Her face pales as she enters the space.

She covers her mouth at the sight—

A giant version of the young man, his head lowered as if in prayer. He crouches on a pile of human skulls—naked—his massive, feathered wings unfurling from his shoulders.

James—a mere speck compared to the giant effigy—kneels at the young man's feet, head bowed in reverence.

Olive swallows hard, calling out to him: "James."

He does not turn or react. He kneels further until he's swallowed by the darkness between the young man's legs.

Just then, a giant wave slams into the side of the hotel.

Windows shatter, doors exploding to mere splinters as emerald seawater crashes into the lobby and floods everything.

Olive climbs on top of the desk as the water begins to rise.

The flood of the apocalypse.

As the water swells, Olive scans the area for higher ground.

The gigantic effigy of the young man vanishes beneath the surface, inhaled by the raging current.

She swims toward the lobby's stairwell, when something beneath the surface pulls at her feet.

She bobs there helplessly for a moment.

Without warning, she's pulled down beneath the surface.

Random pieces of furniture float past her.

She slowly opens her eyes and pales when she sees it—

Milo's body sprawled out against a giant neon-lit crucifix floats in front of her.

Milo's abdomen—slashed, as it was before. Only no blood, this time. His hands—bound to the arms of the cross with cable wire.

The crucifix—a giant cross emanating a blinding neon white light.

Milo's eyes are closed. His head lowered as it was when Olive had first found him.

She swims closer to him. About to reach out and touch him when—

His eyes snap open.

Olive recoils slightly.

Milo smiles at his mother, his face softening.

When he speaks, it's a dim hum echoing beneath the water and shaking her until she can no longer feel anything.

"I've been waiting for you," he whispers.

The neon-lit crucifix shimmers, swallowing both Milo and Olive. The light glows brighter. And brighter.

And brighter until finally the light swallows her whole and she feels nothing.

SEVENTEEN

A bright, sunny day.

Sunlight streams in through the floor-length lobby windows.

Everything is as it was before the massive flood.

Even Olive.

She stands on the hotel's porch for a moment, scanning the empty harbor, when suddenly she notices a steamboat drifting across the horizon.

The vessel—heading toward the island.

Olive races down the front steps. Freezes, realizing she can walk. Looks down and notices her ankle has completely healed.

Shaking her head in bewilderment, she sprints down the pathway toward the island's dock.

The small steamboat pulls into port, blasting its whistle.

The engine slows to a halt as stewards leap from the gangplank and fasten the rigging.

Olive nears the dock, waving at them as they arrive.

But they ignore her.

Moments later, the haggard and bearded ferryman descends the gangplank with boxes filled with food.

Olive approaches him.

"You don't know how happy I am to see you," she says.

The ferryman ignores her, passing the crates to one of the young stewards.

"Bring this up to the cottage," he says. "I expect they'll have a list for you, too."

"We've been trying to call for weeks," Olive says.

The ferryman won't look at her.

"Make sure they have everything they need," he tells the steward. "We won't be coming back for another week."

"There's been a horrible accident," Olive says. "My husband—he's up in the hotel... Are you listening to me—?"

It's then that Olive notices the steward has seen the hotel's front door swinging open.

"Sir. The front door?"

The ferryman sees it.

"Shit," he mutters.

"He needs a doctor right away," Olive says. "Follow me."

The ferryman passes Olive, scaling the pathway toward the hotel's main entrance. The steward follows, hauling the crates of food.

Olive dashes through the front door into the lobby.

The ferryman and the steward arrive not long after, scouring the empty room.

The ferryman studies the door lock.

"No signs of forced entry," he says.

"My husband has a key," Olive explains. "Mr. Patel gave it to him for emergencies."

The steward peers into the lobby's empty gift shop.

"Anything over there—?" the ferryman asks.

"Nothing, sir."

"Please come quick," Olive pleads. "He's in the dining room."

The ferryman walks past Olive, glancing up the lobby's stairwell.

"Anybody up there?" he shouts.

There's no response.

"What are you waiting for—?" Olive asks. "Please. He needs help."

The ferryman and the steward don't react.

"I don't think anyone's here," the steward says.

"Better check the dining room," the ferryman replies.

Olive exhales a sigh of relief. "Yes. Please come quick. This way."

Olive sprints out of the lobby and into the dining room.

She's surprised when she finds the room to be empty. No sign of James or the young man anywhere.

The tables are cleared. No sign of the food they had eaten or the poisoned Cabernet.

"Where is—?"

The ferryman and the steward arrive, scanning the empty room.

"Nothing in here either," the ferryman says.

"No. He was right here," Olive insists. "We have to find him."

"Better check on the folks in the cottage," the ferryman says. "They might know something."

"I'm right here," Olive shouts.

But the ferryman and the steward ignore her, withdrawing from the dining room. Olive follows.

The ferryman and the steward arrive at the small cottage, Olive trailing close behind.

They cover their mouths, coughing, the stench of gas greeting them as soon as they enter.

"Gas. The stove," the ferryman says.

The steward dashes into the kitchen. He turns off the gas stovetop. Then, flings open a window.

"Go check upstairs," the ferryman orders the steward.

The steward ducks out from the living room and hastens up the stairs, Olive chasing after him.

When he arrives at the master bedroom, he finds the room empty. He flings open a window, an ocean breeze filling the room.

"Where are my things—?"

Olive scours the vanity for a sign of any of her belongings. Nothing.

"What happened to all my things—?" she asks, her voice breaking apart.

The steward leans out the door, calling downstairs.

"They're not up here either," he says.

"No. I'm right here," Olive says.

"Better come down," the ferryman shouts. "We'll have to call the police."

"Please. Can't you see me—?" Olive begs.

Olive leaps in front of the steward's path only to have him walk directly through her.

She covers her mouth, realizing.

The steward slips out of the master bedroom and hastens down the stairs.

Olive is left alone, broken.

From the hotel's front porch, Olive watches as another small boat arrives in the harbor. Wind whispers all around her.

She watches as police officers climb onto the dock and are greeted by a somber-faced Mr. Patel.

Olive sits in one of the antique wingback lobby chairs, observing as Mr. Patel is questioned by two police officers.

One of the officers takes notes on a small notepad. The other asks questions.

Mr. Patel shakes his head as if baffled, the sound of his voice muted to Olive as he speaks to them.

She sinks further into the chair, as if she were melting into the furniture.

Later, Olive finds her way to the hotel's attic.

Duvet-covered furniture coated with dust and grime is arranged all over the cramped space.

She sits, looking at her reflection in a mirror.

Suddenly, the young man appears out of thin air, a glorious set of white-feathered wings fanning out from his shoulders.

Olive glares at him for a moment before speaking.

"Are you here to hurt me?" she asks him.

"Can't hurt what's already dead," he tells her.

Olive laughs, amused. "So, it is true."

"Yes—?"

"We go on."

"Sometimes," he tells her. "Not always."

Olive smiles. "They were wrong."

"It's different for everyone."

"And for me—?" Olive asks.

"Yes. You."

"Where's my son—? If I'm dead, shouldn't he be—?" Her voice trails off.

"Your son already crossed over," the young man tells her.

Olive's face scrunches. "Crossed over—?"

"Yes."

"Where to—?"

"To where we go."

"And my husband?" Olive asks, dreading the answer.

"He's gone, too."

"Where—?"

"I was here to help you cross over," the young man explains. "Until you took matters into your own hands... I had every intention of returning you to him. To both of them... But I was told to keep you here."

"For how long—?"

"Until you're ready."

Olive's eyes sparkle wet. "I'm ready. I promise I'm ready."

The young man smiles.

"You will be. One day," he says.

He withdraws, dissolving into the darkness where the two walls meet.

Olive screams, tossing a book at where he was standing.

She slams her fist against the mirror. The glass cracks.

She grabs one of the glistening shards. Holds it against her throat. Swipes it across.

A wound opens, blood fountaining like a geyser. Then, closes.

The blood dries.

Olive slices her throat again.

The same thing happens—a ribbon yawns open and then closes.

She crouches, tossing the shard of glass aside.

She hangs her head in despair like a forgotten child.

Olive makes her way down the path and toward the large boulder overlooking the island's harbor.

"Our Father, who art in heaven, hallowed be thy name; thy kingdom come; thy will be done on earth as it is in heaven."

She arrives at the massive rock, touring it before leaping on top of the boulder.

She sits there quietly, staring out at the sunset.

"Give us this day our daily bread; and forgive us our trespasses as we forgive those who trespass against us…"

Wind whispers all around her, as if it were a gloved hand comforting her and stroking her to sleep.

"And lead us not into temptation but deliver us from evil."

Her eyelids become heavy as she watches the small steamboat drift away until it's swallowed by the horizon.

"For thine is the kingdom, the power, and the glory, for ever and ever."

Olive rubs her hands together, her index finger tracing the outline of the black circle drawn in the center of her open palm.

"Amen," she says.

She sits there, waiting, as more light dims from the sky—the heavens closing their door to her for now.

YOU'LL FIND IT'S LIKE THAT ALL OVER

To say that Gerald Fowler found himself panicked when he uncovered a small fragment of bone buried in the snow near his backyard's vine-draped portico would be a grotesque understatement.

Those in the town of Saint Benedict, New Hampshire who knew full well of Mr. Fowler's fastidiousness could possibly imagine the poor man's dismay at the discovery of such a gruesome offering—how his eyes bulged with concern, how his hands trembled slightly, how the color dimmed from both of his cheeks. Some might have found amusement in the animated, almost melodramatic way in which Mr. Fowler reacted when he first uncovered the thing, but Mr. Fowler considered the situation to be no laughing matter, as was his custom. To him, matters were always far more unpleasant than they actually were.

Of course, at first, Mr. Fowler thought it was some kind of ruse—a horrible prank played on him by some of the younger residents of the neighborhood who were probably getting back at him for not handing out candy at Halloween for the fifth year in a row. He could hardly make sense of why he'd discover a bone in his backyard after the town had been blanketed by the third blizzard of the season. Mr. Fowler was surprised he had even found the thing in the first place.

He had been carefully shoveling the pathway leading to the stone-flanked terrace when something caught his eye— something jutting out of the ground like a piece of piping. He winced when he pulled it from the snow, as if fearful more random parts of human anatomy might sprout from their hiding places too.

Although Mr. Fowler's meticulousness might cause some to mistake him for a doctor or expert surgeon, he was less than adept at identifying the bone as belonging to human or animal. Naturally, he expected it might be more than likely for the bone to belong to some sort of woodland creature, but he couldn't help but allow his mind to consider the frightening possibilities of entertaining the notion that it could possibly be human.

As his thoughts raced with dread-filled scenarios, he twirled the bone between his index finger and his thumb. It was then he realized there was a pair of initials carved into its side—the letter "R" and the letter "P." He squinted, studying each letter closely. His mind immediately turned to his neighbor—an émigré from Bosnia named Rafe Perlzig. He wondered why he thought of Mr. Perlzig almost instantly. After all, Mr. Fowler and his husband had been residents in Saint Benedict for almost as long as he had, and they had hardly spoken to the poor man.

Mr. Fowler's belligerently racist husband had insisted that Mr. Perlzig was driving down the property value of their cul-de-sac and had confided this to multiple of the neighbors they called friends. Of course, Mr. Fowler didn't often listen to his husband, but he loathed himself for considering Mr. Perlzig was behind the prank simply because he was a foreigner. He knew that wasn't the case at all. Mr. Perlzig carried the same initials that were carved into the bone and that was it. It had nothing to do with the fact that he spoke little English or that he hardly waved at them as they drove by in the mornings.

Though he thought of returning inside and letting his husband know of his discovery, Mr. Fowler knew full well if he shared his suspicions of Mr. Perlzig he'd have to endure a litany of accusations and a speech on why immigrants are ruining the country according to his beloved husband. Rather than upset his husband and endure the hate speech, Mr. Fowler buttoned his winter coat, pushed the small piece of bone into his pocket, and marched around the side of the house and toward the main driveway as he headed a few properties down.

The neighborhood was still and quiet as he passed down the narrow lane. Though it was a Sunday, he was astonished that there was so little activity considering the fact that most every household in Saint Benedict attended church regularly. There were no children playing and building snowmen in the front yards. There were no sightings of mothers and fathers snowshoeing or loading their families into idling cars. Of course, there were times when Mr. Fowler lamented the fact that he and his husband were the only queer couple in the neighborhood. Despite that, they had speculated that Mr. Perlzig might be of a similar persuasion given the fact he was a much older man with no spouse and no children.

In fact, as he marched toward Mr. Perlzig's driveway, Mr. Fowler realized he knew so little of him. It was strange to think they had been neighbors for nearly five years and yet most of their passing interactions could be counted on merely one hand. He wondered why his husband despised him so vehemently. Of course, Mr. Perlzig was not necessarily a gifted conversationalist, nor was he an exceptional neighbor by any stretch of the imagination.

But Mr. Fowler knew there was something in his husband's mind when he thought of their neighbor—something unspoken, something unsaid. He couldn't help but wonder if his husband objected to Mr. Perlzig simply out of jealousy. After all, he owned the largest house in the cul-de-sac. Meanwhile, Mr. Fowler and his husband struggled to pay the mortgage on their property on the pittance salary he made as a high school algebra teacher.

As Mr. Fowler turned the corner at Mr. Perlzig's mailbox and began to meander down the tree-flanked corridor leading toward the gentleman's Dutch Colonial house tucked behind a small thicket, he noticed Mr. Perlzig bundled in an overcoat and swinging piles of snow over his shoulder as he shoveled his front pathway.

Mr. Perlzig was an unusual specimen of manhood. He was heavyset enough to be self-conscious about his extra weight, but not so overweight that he attracted unwanted attention. As Mr. Fowler neared him, he took note of the bright orange jacket that Mr. Perlzig wore—tattered and torn, but obviously well-loved and well-worn through the years.

He idled there for a moment, hoping Mr. Perlzig might turn and notice him. But there was no such luck to be had. Mr. Perlzig had his head lowered, hood covering his face, as he labored with each swing of the shovel.

"Beautiful morning, isn't it?" Mr. Fowler said, shoving both hands into his coat pockets.

Mr. Perlzig lifted his head from his work and met Mr. Fowler with a look of bemusement. Always concerned he had overstepped some invisible boundary or that he had carelessly neglected some significant social grace, Mr. Fowler recoiled slightly. He wondered why Mr. Perlzig offered him such a look of discomfort.

"Surely, you didn't come here to discuss the weather," the old man said, his dark moustache twitching like a sleeping caterpillar.

Mr. Fowler hesitated a little, shocked by Mr. Perlzig's frankness. Although many in the neighborhood had come to know of Mr. Perlzig as a man of few words, Mr. Fowler silently mourned the possibility of the formalities of small talk.

"Well, no," he said, trembling as he adjusted his glasses when they slid to the tip of his nose. "I—came over because I found something this morning…"

"Something to move this damn snow," Mr. Perlzig said, tossing the shovel aside so that it slid further down the pathway and skated into the driveway.

Mr. Fowler fished inside his coat pocket and pulled out the small piece of bone, brandishing it in the sunlight so that Mr. Perlzig could see the gruesome little offering.

"I found it buried in my backyard," Mr. Fowler explained, cautious of each and every word. "I thought maybe—"

"You thought I had left it there for you to find," Mr. Perlzig interrupted, a smile warming with redness across his face like a spring thaw.

"Well, no. I never meant to imply anything," Mr. Fowler said. "But there's a pair of initials carved into the bone. Your initials."

Mr. Fowler passed the small bone fragment into Mr. Perlzig's gloved hands. He watched in silence as Mr. Perlzig studied the bone with such scrupulousness.

"And you interpreted these initials as an invitation to come here and harass an old man," Mr. Perlzig said.

Mr. Fowler sensed his limbs tighten; his chest squeezed a little as he labored with every breath. "I assure you. I never meant to—"

"You're right," the old man said. "It was an invitation."

Mr. Fowler squinted, wondering if he had heard Mr. Perlzig correctly. Had he really intended this small piece of bone to serve as some sort of grim summons? Against his better judgment, Mr. Fowler inched forward toward the old man.

"I was hoping either you or your husband might come by," Mr. Perlzig said, winking at him.

Mr. Fowler could hardly believe it to be true. "You left it there for us to find?"

"Are you a gambling man, Mr. Fowler?" the old man asked, tossing the bone up in the air and catching it with the same hand. "I once made a bet about the time and place of my father's death. Hodgkin's lymphoma. Awful disease. Then, when I was certain I would win, I bet against myself. After all, there's no fun in winning all the time. I win only when I need to—when it's a necessity."

Mr. Fowler swallowed hard. "A necessity?"

"Like today, for instance," Mr. Perlzig said. "If I made a bet with you, would you bet that I would need to win?"

Mr. Fowler considered it for a moment. "Given the fact you went to all this trouble, I would say yes."

"You're a natural gambler," Mr. Perlzig said. "Well done. You'd win in this case."

But Mr. Fowler was less than comforted. The question still rattled in his mind like a small pebble in an empty tin can: *To whom does the bone belong?*

Before Mr. Fowler could ask, Mr. Perlzig was leading him down the pathway and toward the small snow-covered black Volvo parked in the corner of the driveway.

"What do you say we make another bet?" Mr. Perlzig asked, pocketing the bone fragment. "I'll bet you five hundred dollars that you can't clean the snow from my car in under three minutes."

Mr. Fowler eyed the car as it sat without movement in the far corner of the driveway. It was a small vehicle, of course, but it was covered with more than seven inches of snowfall, Mr. Fowler guessed. He was spry, but he was still doubtful he could clean the entire vehicle in under three minutes. More to the point, he wondered why Mr. Perlzig had gone out of his way to bait him into a game of betting. He and his husband hadn't interacted with him at all in the five years they had been neighbors. Why now?

That's precisely what Mr. Fowler asked Mr. Perlzig.

"Why are you asking me to do this?" he said to him.

Mr. Perlzig paled and shook his head, as if insulted.

"Does it matter?" the old man replied. "You're here now. What do you say?"

Mr. Fowler couldn't be certain. He wasn't the betting type. Of course, would he bet on his life that he and his racist husband would eventually go their separate ways? Absolutely. To Mr. Perlzig's point, did it really matter why he had sought him out for a game of betting? Mr. Fowler conceded he was at least a little curious of the whole ordeal. Not to mention, money had always been an issue between him and his husband. He wondered if Mr. Perlzig somehow knew that.

Mr. Fowler hesitated. He sensed his throat squeeze tight to the point where every inhale and exhale was hard labor.

"I don't expect you to have the money on you right now," Mr. Perlzig said, opening his wallet and pulling out five hundred-dollar bills. "But I want you to know that I'm good for it." Mr. Fowler knew that the old man was more than good for the bet. After all, he was the homeowner on the street who had paid in cash when he first purchased his house. Mr. Fowler figured that Mr. Perlzig must be sitting on a small fortune.

"Do we have a deal?" the old man asked, extending his hand for Mr. Fowler to shake.

Mr. Fowler thought for a moment. Of course, there was every possibility he'd lose. But the thrill of the bet made it seem so exciting to him. For a moment, he wasn't reminded of his loveless marriage. He wasn't preoccupied with the needs of his students. He was simply a man of his own destiny and eager to make good on the bet.

Mr. Fowler took Mr. Perlzig's hand, and they shook.

After Mr. Perlzig passed Mr. Fowler a small broom, Mr. Perlzig explained that he would keep time on his watch and expect the car to be fully cleaned by the time three minutes had passed. When Mr. Perlzig saw the minute hand click over to the next number, he gestured to Mr. Fowler to begin.

Mr. Fowler took the broom and began beating it against the car as cakes of snow fell to the ground in thick, cottony clumps. He circled the vehicle, beating hard against the snow and knocking off more and more as he raced from the taillights to the headlights. Occasionally, he'd glance at Mr. Perlzig or notice him in his peripheral vision and would see the old man hold up a finger as if to signify that one minute had passed. Mr. Fowler sensed his heart beating like a hammer against a rock and wondered if it might fly right out of his chest. He circled the car again, patting the snow from the car's roof and brushing off all he could reach.

Mr. Fowler glanced at Mr. Perlzig. Another minute had passed. He only had a minute left, and he knew if he wanted to win, he had to make the last few moments count. Brushing the snow from the hood and the windshield, Mr. Fowler tirelessly beat against the car until the snow was wiped clean. Just as he scrubbed the snow caked onto the vehicle's front grille, Mr. Perlzig shouted that time was up and for Mr. Fowler to drop his broom.

Mr. Fowler leaned against the car, panting violently like a cat in heat. He hadn't worked so diligently, so assiduously, since he was a young boy and he would visit his grandmother and grandfather at their farm in Vermont.

"You'll scratch the paint," Mr. Perlzig warned him as he circled the car, inspecting every inch of the freshly cleaned vehicle.

Mr. Fowler's eyes followed him, watching the old man as he scanned the car while carefully avoiding the piles of snow he had pushed to the ground.

"Well?" Mr. Fowler said, the suspense almost too much for him to bear.

Mr. Perlzig folded his arms. "It looks—perfect. I couldn't have done a better job myself."

"I won?"

Mr. Perlzig merely nodded.

Before Mr. Fowler could respond, Mr. Perlzig took his head between his hands and kissed him on both cheeks.

"Well done," the old man said. "But I bet you'd fancy another bet."

Mr. Fowler steadied his breathing, choking on his saliva. "Another bet?"

"You can't walk away after merely one bet," Mr. Perlzig explained. "That's not fair to either party."

Mr. Fowler supposed the old man was right. But he couldn't imagine what else they might be able to bet.

Mr. Perlzig led Mr. Fowler up the pathway toward the house's massive front door outfitted with various locks and latches.

"Now, this time I know you won't beat me," Mr. Perlzig said, pulling a small key from his coat pocket and pressing it into Mr. Fowler's open palm. "I've timed how long it takes to successfully unlock each and every latch on this door. It takes precisely forty-five seconds. I'll bet you can't do it in under thirty seconds."

Mr. Fowler frowned. This is where he would draw the line, if ever. "That doesn't seem like a fair bet to me," he said. "You have the advantage of knowing how long it takes."

"True," Mr. Perlzig conceded, folding his arms. "But if you're successful, I'll pay you a thousand dollars in cash.

If you lose, I'll merely expect you to return the five hundred dollars to me."

Mr. Fowler thought for a moment. "That's all I'd have to return? Just the five hundred?"

He had to admit it wasn't much of a gamble. Of course, if he lost, he'd be right back where he started. Then again, if he won, he'd be flushed with fifteen hundred dollars' worth of cash. His husband certainly wouldn't complain much then. At least not for a month or so.

Mr. Fowler gripped the key in his hand and readied himself in front of the door's top lock. He glanced at Mr. Perlzig for when to begin, Mr. Perlzig's eyes trained on his watch and waiting. Finally, the old man signaled to Mr. Fowler and the race was on. Mr. Fowler pushed the key into the first lock, twisting it a bit before hearing the latch come undone. Then, he pushed the key into another lock and undid that one with the same force he had conjured for the first lock. Out of his peripheral vision, he saw Mr. Perlzig carefully monitoring the time with his wristwatch. Mr. Perlzig's expression shifted to something dire, as if it were an indication that the seconds were quickly running out and that Mr. Fowler would not complete the assignment in time.

As Mr. Fowler fumbled with another lock, the key slid from his grip and landed on the ground. Mr. Fowler bent down, swiping his hands and preparing them for work again. Without hesitation, Mr. Fowler pushed the key into the final lock and twisted it until he heard the door pop open slightly. Pushing down on the handle, Mr. Fowler eased the door open right as Mr. Perlzig signaled that time was up.

Mr. Fowler glanced back at Mr. Perlzig and found an expression of bewilderment—perhaps even a semblance of dismay—had made its home across his face.

"Well done," the old man said.

From his tone, Mr. Fowler couldn't tell if Mr. Perlzig was genuinely pleased or exasperated with him. But he wasn't too keen on suffering the ordeal any longer to find out.

"The money," Mr. Fowler said.

"You'd deny an old man the pleasure of your company?" Mr. Perlzig asked. "Certainly, you'll come inside for tea before you leave."

Although Mr. Fowler had excuses at the ready, all seemed inconsequential or hollow. He naturally couldn't play the role of an impertinent house guest and knew that any shortcomings of politeness might make it unbearable to remain as Mr. Perlzig's neighbor for another five years. If he had that long to live, that is.

Without uttering a word, Mr. Fowler followed the old man into the house and through the drawing room where a small serviette of tea had already been arranged. Mr. Fowler looked around the room and couldn't help but take inventory of the vast collection of antique appliances Mr. Perlzig had collected over the years. All items were neatly shined, as if recently polished, and glittering like precious gemstones in the light. Mr. Fowler felt it was odd to find such painstaking care went into tending to the antiques pinned to the walls and arranged in the corners of rooms while the rest of the house remained in such a state of disarray.

As he circled the dust-covered sofa, Mr. Fowler noticed a large chalkboard near the fireplace. On the chalkboard were various pictures and letters placed in a seemingly random order.

"What's that?" he asked, easing onto the sofa.

"That's going to be our next bet," Mr. Perlzig explained, pouring a cup of tea and passing it to Mr. Fowler. "I'll bet you can't solve the expression in one guess."

"Expression?"

Mr. Perlzig leapt out of his chair and crossed the room, dragging the chalkboard closer for Mr. Fowler to see. "Each of these pictures and letters make up a word. The entire board contains a hidden expression that you have to guess."

Mr. Fowler was tired. He could scarcely keep his eyes open, let alone solve an expression made up entirely of pictures and letters.

"I think this is where I'll see myself out," he said, straightening from the couch and heading toward the door.

"I'll double your existing winnings," Mr. Perlzig exclaimed, calling after him. "That's three thousand dollars."

Mr. Fowler halted as if his shoes were suddenly filled with concrete. He turned slightly, facing Mr. Perlzig.

"Three thousand?" he asked.

Mr. Perlzig nodded.

"In cash," the old man added.

Of course, Mr. Fowler could have turned him down, could have told him that he had done enough gambling for the day and would take his winnings elsewhere. But politeness got the better of him once more. He had been instilled with the refinement of a young lady at her first cotillion thanks to his mother's constant supervision when he was younger. In fact, his husband often berated him and referred to him as lacking proper male anatomy when Mr. Fowler was feeling particularly sentimental or overly cautious.

In a mere gesture that let Mr. Perlzig know he was willing to play his game, Mr. Fowler resumed his seat on the sofa and glared at the first image on the chalkboard: a small wooden log embellished with a scarlet ribbon and a wreath made of ivy.

"So, the first picture—it's a log decorated like Christmastime," he said, squinting as he studied the depiction.

His eyes darted to Mr. Perlzig for a look of approval, but the old man would neither confirm nor deny it.

Mr. Fowler thought more. Finally, it came to him: "A Yule log."

Mr. Perlzig merely smiled.

"So, the first word is Yule."

Then Mr. Fowler moved on to the second clue: the letter "F," a plus symbol, and a picture of a pair of eyes.

"The letter 'F' plus a pair of eyes," he whispered, adjusting his glasses to see better. "F-plus-eye. F-eye."

Once again, it came to him: "Find."

Mr. Perlzig applauded. "Very good, Mr. Fowler. You're a natural."

Mr. Fowler moved on to the third clue: a human face covered with acne, preceded by a minus symbol and the letter "Z."

"Zits," he said. "But the word 'zits' without the letter 'Z' is the word 'it's'. So, the phrase so far is: *You'll find it's…*"

If Mr. Fowler wanted a modicum of praise this time, he would go wanting. Mr. Perlzig merely sipped from his teacup and ordered Mr. Fowler to continue.

Mr. Fowler moved on to the next clue: a picture of a lake with the silhouettes of large mountains in the background.

"Lake," he said beneath his breath, his eyes going over the picture again and again. He glanced at Mr. Perlzig who immediately answered with a look of disapproval. "Or a word that sounds like 'lake,'" Mr. Fowler said gently.

He thought for a moment. The word crashed into his mind: "like."

"You'll find it's like…"

Mr. Perlzig winced slightly, noticeably hiding the fact he was so impressed with Mr. Fowler's deductive abilities.

Mr. Fowler's eyes drifted to the next image: a picture of a gentleman's top hat preceded by the letter "T" and a plus symbol.

"Top hat," Mr. Fowler said. "Or just a hat. The word 'hat' plus the letter 'T.' THAT. *You'll find it's like that…*"

Once again, Mr. Perlzig showed little to no expression. He was far too enraptured in the thrill of the game, easing onto the edge of his seat and nearly spilling his tea as he brought the rim of the cup to his quivering lips.

Mr. Fowler moved on to the next illustration: a picture of a soccer ball followed by the letter "B" and a minus symbol.

"Ball," he said. "Minus the letter 'B.' ALL. *You'll find it's like that all…*"

Finally, he came upon the seventh and final clue: a small picture of the globe. His eyes flashed to Mr. Perlzig for an explanation, but the old man wouldn't divulge his secret.

"You'll find it's like that all earth," Mr. Fowler said insincerely.

Mr. Perlzig squinted at him. "Is that your official guess?"

But Mr. Fowler knew that wasn't right. It certainly wasn't an expression he had heard before. He knew it had to be something else. Suddenly, the word "over" pushed itself to the front door of his thoughts.

"All over," he blurted out.

Mr. Perlzig froze at Mr. Fowler's discovery.

"You'll find it's like that all over," Mr. Fowler said.

Mr. Perlzig's face thawed with another smile. "You've been brilliant, Mr. Fowler. Well done."

Mr. Fowler's praise was short lived, however. The phrase elbowed its way through the brawn of his thoughts—*You'll find it's like that all over.* It perplexed him, haunted him even.

"What's it like?" Mr. Fowler asked the old man.

Mr. Perlzig answered with merely a silent look of confusion.

"What's it like all over? What does it mean?"

Mr. Perlzig laughed, as if genuinely amused. "You know how people are. So eager to disguise their pain. So willing to maintain social graces and remain polite even in the face of discomfort."

Mr. Fowler thought for a moment. Of course, there was some truth to what Mr. Perlzig had said. After all, there were many opportunities for him to leave, for him to say he'd had enough with the betting, and yet he remained. Mr. Fowler realized he had masqueraded his discomfort as politeness simply because it had been expected of him. He wondered to what extent Mr. Perlzig might use him if the old man had known this—if the old man had known to just what extent Mr. Fowler would go to please him and maintain all social graces.

"I probably should be going," Mr. Fowler said, lifting himself off the sofa and eyeing the exit door.

"Not before we make our final bet," Mr. Perlzig said.

Mr. Fowler felt warmness heat in both of his cheeks. "My husband will be wondering where I went. I wouldn't want to keep him waiting."

"Be polite," Mr. Perlzig said. "You should be a gentleman."

There it was again—the way in which Mr. Perlzig played Mr. Fowler like an accordion. Mr. Fowler knew it and recognized it, but there was nothing he could do about it. After all, Mr. Perlzig would continue to be their neighbor for the foreseeable future, and he so desperately wanted matters to remain civilized between the separate households.

Reluctantly, Mr. Fowler followed Mr. Perlzig up the stairs toward the attic door. As he ascended, he counted each and every step. Mr. Fowler, forever gifted with the brain of a mathematician, invented various mathematical problems to solve just to keep his mind occupied, just to keep him from falling apart as he followed Mr. Perlzig into the small attic cramped with sheet-covered furniture. It was then that Mr. Fowler sensed himself pale when he saw the room's ornate centerpiece: an eighteenth-century guillotine—the impressively massive framework made from red-painted wood, the blade glistening at Mr. Fowler and whispering a wordless threat as it glinted in the light.

"Stunning, isn't it?" Mr. Perlzig said, circling the machine. "I won it in an auction in Strasbourg."

For Mr. Fowler, the word "stunning" didn't seem to do the contraption justice. His eyes drifted from the elaborately designed crossbar at the helm of the device down to the lunette where convicts' heads were once positioned before the mouton was released and the blade was sent crashing down. It was then that Mr. Fowler's heart sank when he wondered why Mr. Perlzig was so adamant on showing him this device.

"I'd like to make a wager with you," Mr. Perlzig said, brandishing a neatly polished pair of antique handcuffs he had retrieved from a nearby bureau. "A wager that will decide the matter of who is the better man. I'll bet that you can't undo these handcuffs in under fifteen seconds."

Mr. Fowler studied the handcuffs as Mr. Perlzig passed them from hand to hand.

"This is a trick?" he asked.

"Nonsense," the old man assured him, presenting him with a small key made of brass. "This is the key right here. I'll give it to you before I even begin keeping track of the time." But something about the presentation of the whole bet didn't sit well with Mr. Fowler.

"What do I have to do?" he asked him.

"You'll allow me to handcuff you while you slide your head through the contraption here," Mr. Perlzig explained. "If you remove the handcuffs and escape the device in under fifteen seconds, I will pay you one hundred thousand dollars."

Mr. Fowler stalled for a moment. He could scarcely believe his ears. Had he heard him correctly, after all? One hundred thousand dollars was more than he made in a year at the local high school.

"And if I lose?" Mr. Fowler asked.

Mr. Perlzig chuckled, as if genuinely amused. "If you lose, you'll be dead, my friend."

Mr. Fowler's eyes drifted up to the blade as it swung there from its special mount. He winced slightly, pushing his index finger inside his ear as if to sponge away the name he kept hearing being whispered as the blade glared down at him.

Against his better judgment, Mr. Fowler agreed to Mr. Perlzig's bet.

"Wonderful," the old man exclaimed. "Now, let's get you prepared for the big moment." As Mr. Perlzig guided him over to the guillotine, Mr. Fowler felt uncomfortable in his arms as if he were being embraced by some predatory insect. He cringed a little as Mr. Perlzig instructed him to kneel down and slide his head through the lunette. Mr. Fowler obeyed without comment, craning his head through the device and staring down at the small basket arranged below him to capture his head if he lost the bet. Of course, he hoped the basket would be unnecessary, but there was a part of him that remained unsure.

Once Mr. Fowler had been secured, Mr. Perlzig grabbed his hands and locked them in the handcuffs behind his back. Then he passed the key into Mr. Fowler's open palm.

"You're not to use the key until I begin the countdown," the old man instructed. Mr. Fowler nodded.

Mr. Perlzig circled the device until he was in Mr. Fowler's limited eyeline.

"You're ready?" Mr. Perlzig asked.

Mr. Fowler swallowed nervously, twirling the key between his thumb and index finger.

"Yes."

Mr. Perlzig glanced at his wristwatch and smiled. "Begin."

Mr. Fowler pinched the key between his fingers and struggled to locate the first lock to undo. He stabbed at the handcuffs with the small key, tirelessly searching for the small opening. Just as he located the lock, the key slipped from his sweating hands and skated across the floor toward Mr. Perlzig's feet. Mr. Fowler sensed himself tighten, as if the hand of an invisible deity were squeezing him to death.

"I dropped it," he exclaimed.

"Ten seconds left," Mr. Perlzig announced, nearing the guillotine with intent.

Mr. Fowler thrashed helplessly like a trout caught in a fisherman's net. He sensed the hairs on the back of his neck curl and then straighten.

"Give me the key," he shouted to the old man.

Mr. Perlzig begin to announce the countdown number by number: "*Five... four... three...*"

Just as Mr. Perlzig reached the final number, he dragged down the release handle in one swift pull. The blade released, sliding down and landing only mere inches away from Mr. Fowler's precious neck.

When he opened his eyes, he saw Mr. Perlzig leering over him and laughing. It was then Mr. Perlzig pulled a lever and cranked the blade until it was secured in its ornate rigging.

Mr. Fowler screamed for help, but it was no use.

Mr. Fowler's lips quivered, unsure what to say. He sensed a warmness collect between his legs and begin to trickle down his ankles. His whole body trembled, uncertain whether he was alive or dead. The sensation of Mr. Perlzig undoing the handcuffs and dragging him from his knees told him that he was still alive—barely.

"Can you move?" Mr. Perlzig asked him, propping Mr. Fowler's body against him for support. "You're OK."

The sound of Mr. Perlzig's voice was so muted that to Mr. Fowler it sounded as if the old man were gently speaking to him underwater.

"Perhaps some tea before you go?" Mr. Perlzig asked him, guiding him toward the attic door.

Mr. Fowler, still in a daze, glanced up at the guillotine's blade again, as if wondering if he had dreamed the entire ordeal.

"It wasn't real," Mr. Fowler whispered. "None of it was real."

Whether he said it for himself to realize or to condemn Mr. Perlzig, he couldn't be positive. Then, of course, there was the nauseating question that nagged at him, that kept him wondering:

"Why me?"

Mr. Perlzig's face softened slightly.

"Because I knew you'd come," the old man said. "They always come, after all. People are alike all over. You'll find that out."

Although Mr. Perlzig insisted on sharing another cup of tea with Mr. Fowler before he left, it was an invitation Mr. Fowler would never accept. Not only was his husband probably wondering to where he had run off, but he could hardly bear another second in the clothes he was wearing.

Before Mr. Fowler left, Mr. Perlzig handed him the small bone he had found earlier.

"Whose bone is this?" Mr. Fowler asked him.

It wasn't that he wanted to know, he desperately *needed* to know. He knew he wouldn't be able to sleep until he knew to whom the bone belonged.

"Think of it as a gift," Mr. Perlzig told him. "You wouldn't want to be rude, after all. Would you?"

Of course, Mr. Fowler wouldn't. He had been taught not to.

As Mr. Fowler ambled home, doing his best to conceal the dark stain blooming between his legs, he thought of Mr. Perlzig and realized the old man was right. People are so desperate to not offend, to maintain social graces even in the most unusual circumstances. Mr. Fowler wondered if perhaps Mr. Perlzig had targeted him because he had known that. There were many things Mr. Fowler wondered when he reflected on his suffering.

What was certain was that people are indeed alike all over, meaning that if others had been harassed and mercilessly taunted by Mr. Perlzig's bets, they certainly weren't coming forward out of sheer embarrassment. Mr. Fowler conceded he was humiliated. He never wanted to speak of the wagers he had made with Mr. Perlzig. Whether he was fearful of reliving the trauma of that day or simply because he chose to quarter it away in the darkest recesses of his mind, Mr. Fowler was uncertain.

Things became a little clearer in the summer months when the neighborhood hosted a small gathering in the local park. While children played croquet with their parents, Mr. Fowler and his husband merely observed the festivities like outsiders, as was their custom. Of course, Mr. Perlzig was not there. However, the specter of his presence lingered over the picnic like the dim vapor from a distant car's engine.

While Mr. Fowler approached the nearby picnic table sprawling with trays and containers of warm food others had brought, he accidentally bumped into a gentleman who was entirely new to him. The gentleman was short with thinning dark red hair and a pockmarked face. When Mr. Fowler asked him how he was invited to the picnic, the gentleman told him how he and his husband had recently moved into the neighborhood.

Things became even stranger when the gentleman leaned down and dropped a small bone fragment from his shirt pocket. Mr. Fowler watched as the gentleman frantically swiped it from the ground and pocketed it almost immediately. In the few seconds Mr. Fowler had seen the bone, he noticed a pair of initials carved into the side: the letter "R" and the letter "P."

It was then that Mr. Fowler realized that he and the young gentleman had much to talk about.

AFTERWORD

When I was very little, I desperately wanted to believe in God.

My parents were somewhat devout and made certain we were smartly dressed and prepared for Sunday service at 10 a.m. at our town's congregational church. Many of my happiest childhood memories were in that church, if I'm being totally truthful. I was awkward as a child and, therefore, prone to isolating myself from others. I found no camaraderie, no sense of companionship in children my own age. In fact, I felt most comfortable around adults. Other children found me quite strange and deemed me too bizarre to invite to their playground activities. Granted, my interests were eclectic for a child, and I often found myself longing to make a connection with someone, something, simply because that's a very human desire, a basic human want—to form a bond with someone else.

Since I typically wasn't included in activities hosted by my peers, I often invented my own amusement. It was during these formative years that I first developed an infatuation with reading and then later the art of writing. That said, the community and the sanctity of our town's church was so deeply integral to the lives of my parents, I wanted to find meaning in what they found important. I wanted to believe in God more than anything. My mother's faith inspired me and made me envious at times—seeing how content she was at her place in the cosmos, her understanding of things, her acceptance of what she could never change. I wanted that same comfort, that same connection that I thought was possible only through God.

Though I strained to find meaning in religion, I found myself turning up empty-handed. It was virtually impossible for me to believe. Though I admired the idea of a divine creator, I could scarcely convince myself to accept something so fantastical, so absurd. I wanted to believe in God, but every bit of reasoning within me told me that it was never meant to be.

I can still so distinctly recall the moment when I came to terms with that fact—when I knew unequivocally that I did not possess the same faith that my mother and father held. It was a truly frightening moment. Not only was I different from the children around me, but I was decidedly different from the people who raised me. I felt like an alien—an otherworldly creature that should be studied. In my despair, I realized what I wanted more than anything—I wanted to connect with something. I wanted to make a connection and form a bond that would last a lifetime.

That desire—that indescribable itch to connect with someone, something—is fixed at the very heart of *Things Have Gotten Worse Since We Last Spoke and Other Misfortunes*. Though the stories in this collection are decidedly different from one another, they are tethered by the human need to connect with someone, something else.

In the collection's titular novella, the character Agnes is desperate to find companionship in another. The novella is essentially about the lengths a person might be willing to go in order to satisfy their loved one, in order to keep their beloved from leaving.

In *The Enchantment*, the character Olive is filled with the same level of desperation. This time, however, her fixation is her faith. Not only does she want to rekindle a connection with her estranged husband, but she greatly wants to believe in the afterlife.

Finally, in "You'll Find It's Like That All Over," the character of Mr. Fowler is fervent in his desire to stay in good graces with his eccentric neighbor. His politeness is tested when things become sordid, and despite these moments where he hesitates, he remains steadfast because he wants to maintain his connection to Mr. Perlzig.

This collection of macabre tales is my attempt at making sense of some of the connections I've missed or forsaken over the years. Religion and faith play a huge component in some of these stories as I continue to struggle with the fact that I still cannot reasonably believe in a divine creator. Of course, I admire the dedication of others; however, the connection and balance that faith presumably provides is still lost on me. To me, there is nothing but oblivion waiting for us at the end of our journeys here on Earth. My mother promises me that we'll see one another again when we pass on.

I don't know if I believe her.

That's what truly scares me.

Eric LaRocca

Boston, MA
26 January 2022

ACKNOWLEDGMENTS

First and foremost, my heartfelt gratitude belongs to Editor Extraordinaire Cath Trechman of Titan Books for believing in my work. This book would not have been possible without her faith in me as a storyteller. To that end, I would like to thank the entire Titan Books team. More specifically, I would like to thank Lydia Gittins, Katharine Carroll, and Kabriya Coghlan for their persistence, diligence, and kindness.

I would be remiss if I did not take this opportunity to thank our fabulous cover artist, Julia Lloyd, for creating such magnificent and dynamic artwork for our cover.

My gratitude also belongs to my hard working and incredible literary agent, Priya Doraswamy of Lotus Lane Literary Agency.

Huge thanks to my Film/TV manager, Ryan Lewis, for always believing in me.

Lastly, my eternal gratitude to my partner, Ali, for loving me unconditionally and showing me the many reasons why I should love and respect myself.

ABOUT THE AUTHOR

ERIC LAROCCA (he/they) is the Bram Stoker Award®-nominated and Splatterpunk Award-winning author of the viral sensation, *Things Have Gotten Worse Since We Last Spoke*. A lover of luxury fashion and an admirer of European musical theatre, Eric can often be found roaming the streets of his home city, Boston, MA, for inspiration. For more information, please visit ericlarocca.com.

For more fantastic fiction, author events,
exclusive excerpts, competitions, limited editions and more

VISIT OUR WEBSITE
titanbooks.com

LIKE US ON FACEBOOK
facebook.com/titanbooks

FOLLOW US ON TWITTER AND INSTAGRAM
@TitanBooks

EMAIL US
readerfeedback@titanemail.com